DEATH—IN LIVING COLOR

Blood was running down Foster's chin from a busted lip. He placed his hands together and looked up into the glass eye of the camera. Closing his eyes for a moment, he asked God to give him strength to do this.

"Mr. Ambassador, please! Please help us. We—"

"No!" screamed Watson as he saw the pistol suddenly appear in Arias's hand and move toward the back of Foster's head. The sound of the gun exploding in the small room drowned out the rest of his cry.

Foster pitched forward to the floor. The cameraman cursed. Blood and brains from the chunk of skull that had been blown out of the right side of the boy's head had splattered onto the lens. Arias was laughing sadistically as he said, "Even special effects. What more could they want?"

Berkley Books by James N. Pruitt

The SPECIAL OPERATIONS COMMAND Series

INTRODUCTION

United States Special Operations Command

The United States Special Operations Command (USSO-COM) is one of eight unified or joint service commands in the U.S. military's combatant command structure. It was officially established as a major part of America's defense system on April 16, 1987.

USSOCOM prepares assigned forces to carry out special operations, psychological operations, and civil affairs missions as required and, if directed by the president or secretary of defense, plans for and conducts special operations.

In addition to Korea and Vietnam, the U.S. has been involved through its Special Action Forces in literally dozens of conflicts throughout the world. The principal strategies employed by the enemies of the U.S. in these conflicts were either revolutionary (guerrilla) warfare or terrorism.

Over the years, a corps of specialists developed within the U.S. military system. Because the military establishment has viewed these Special Forces as a threat to their power and appropriations, they actively opposed the organization of this highly trained and proficient corps of specialists. This corps consisted of the Special Forces (the Green Berets) and the Rangers, plus certain aviation units in the Army, the Air

Commandos, the 1st Special Operations Wing of the Air Force, and the Navy SEALs.

With the rise of terrorism, the Special Operations Forces received a high public profile. Because the public was so impressed by this new form of warfare, the State Department and the Pentagon could neither ignore nor suppress the response capabilities of these Special Forces.

Ten years ago, a career in Special Operations in any of the services was a dead end. It was career field to be avoided by anyone who wished to retire above the grade of lieutenant colonel. However, a powerful political constituency in Congress has forced a change in the situation. All Special Operations Forces are now pooled under one joint command at MacDill Air Force Base, Tampa Bay, Florida. The Special Operations Command has all its forces under one three-star general. These forces are charged with the mission of performing special operations at the direction of the president anywhere in the world.

This series is dedicated to the men and women of USSO-COM whose sacrifices for the honor of their country shall stand as an inspiration for all time. God bless them all.

Bobbie J. Mattson: Know as B.J. to his friends, Mattson served as an NCO Green Beret medic in Vietnam. As a Distinguished Military Graduate of Texas A&M after the war, he accepted a regular commission and returned to Special Forces. His vast experience in Special Operations has earned him the honor of serving as the SOCOM commander's handpicked operative on all high-level missions ordered by the White House.

That honor has taken its toll on his family. A marriage of sixteen years now teeters on the brink. He stands at the crossroads, unable to choose between his marriage and SO-COM. In the shadows is a troubled world, racked with wars, drugs, and terrorism, which refuses to wait for his decision.

Lieutenant Commander Jacob Winfield Mortimer IV: A Navy SEAL who is eight years younger than Mattson, Jake is the scion of a Philadelphia main line family. His father heads a law firm that is internationally known and highly respected. As a graduate of Harvard, Jake was expected to become a member of the firm. But being stuck behind a desk was not his cup of tea. He has made his career in Special Operations as commander of SEAL Team 6, the naval component of Delta Force. Jake is a devil with the ladies, a wild man who will do virtually anything to accomplish his mission. It was this determination that made him the SOCOM commander's choice as B. J. Mattson's partner.

Lieutenant General Jonathan J. Johnson: A United States Air Force officer and commander of SOCOM, Johnson was personally selected by the president to lead the elite unit. An old Spectre Gunship pilot from the Vietnam era, "Q-Tip" Johnson is a second-generation fighter jock. He flew fighters in Vietnam, and Spectres over Grenada. A firm believer in Special Operations, he utilizes Mattson and Mortimer as his watchdogs during important missions, a decision that has already proven to be a wise one following missions in Ecuador, Burma, and Chad. Johnson's faith in his two top-notch troubleshooters is exemplified by his standing order to both officers: "You are authorized to take any and all actions you deem necessary to accomplish the mission."

Major General Raymond Sweet: A conventional twit, assigned by the Pentagon as Johnson's deputy, his real purpose is to spy on the command and, if possible, give ammunition to its enemies in order to have the unit disbanded.

CHAPTER 1

0015 hours—June 9, 1990
Brazil

Humid night air hung over the small Brazilian town of Boa Vista like a wet invisible curtain. The cobblestone streets were deserted. It was well after midnight, and the weary people of Boa Vista had retreated to their beds or straw mats, exhausted, following their normal sixteen-hour workday.

Colonel Nikolai Molotov wiped the sweat from his brow. The small alleyway where he stood was close and no air moved. This made the night even move unbearable. Lifting the cover from the face of his watch, he checked the time. His contact was late. Keeping his back pressed to the wall, he peered out of the darkness and reaffirmed the location of two personal bodyguards who had taken up positions in the small plaza across the street.

To the untrained eye, the small park, bathed in the bright glow of a full moon, appeared unoccupied. That was as it should be. The two bodyguards had been handpicked by Molotov from the forces of the Spetsnaz, Russia's elite special warfare unit. The Spetsnaz was the equivalent of America's Green Berets and the crack antiterrorist unit, the Delta Force. They were the best of the best the Russians had to offer. Molotov should know. He, himself, had been one of the creators of the Special Action school where the unit was trained.

Leaning his head back against the warm bricks, he closed his tired eyes. Over the past seventy-two hours, sleep had only come in bits and pieces; an hour here, thirty minutes there. That had sufficed to bring him to this point in his mission. But now, the Soviet colonel could feel the lack of sleep beginning to take its toll on him. Considering that Molotov was fifty-eight years old, he had done remarkably well to make it this far. But such was the nature of this man who still carried himself well on his six-foot-two, stocky frame. Absent were the potbelly and rolls of flab hanging over the sides of his tightly belted waistline. If one were to judge Molotov's age by his physique, he would assume the man to be in his early forties. Not until one saw his face would he realize his mistake.

It was a strong face, the type that could draw your attention, even in a crowd; weatherworn and slightly wrinkled, showing a lifetime of experience. His hair was black with faint streaks of silver along the sides. His eyes were as dark as his hair, deep and penetrating, almost hypnotic in their sharpness. His jaw was wide and square, and his broad shoulders had carried a lifetime of burdens.

Born in the winter of 1931, Molotov's very existence had begun in the harsh, bitter cold of the Ukraine. The fifth son of a poor peasant farmer, he learned quickly that the key to survival was strength and determination. The weak were destined to perish. He had not reached his teens before he learned the meaning of war. The Germans swarmed down on his small village and slaughtered all but a few children who had hidden in the fields. Molotov lost his family, his home, and the chance of a normal childhood that day. By the age of twelve, Molotov was a member of the Russian resistance. On his thirteenth birthday he killed his first man. He seemed a natural at the art of guerrilla warfare. By the war's end, he had lost count of the number of men who had fallen before his deadly accuracy with a rifle or those who had felt the sting of his razor sharp knife.

Recognizing the young Molotov's natural adaptability to war, the motherland raised him into manhood through the finest military schools. A Soviet officer by the age of twenty-four, Molotov had served his country well. From the cold of East Germany to the steaming heat of the jungles of Vietnam; from the barren rock-strewn mountains of Afghanistan to the tropical rain forests of Central and South America, he had never questioned his country's objectives or voiced an opinion contrary to policy. He was a soldier, not a political puppet. There was no medal or honor that had not been bestowed on him by a grateful nation. He had been offered promotion to general on a number of occasions, but gracefully declined the offers because that would mean relinquishing the command of his beloved Spetsnaz. To the people of Russia, Nikolai Molotov had achieved legendary status as a true hero and patriot of the motherland.

Standing silently in the dark, odor-filled alleyway of a small town in Brazil, he wondered if the people would still consider him a hero when this affair was over.

The sound of hard-soled shoes walking on the cobblestones echoed lightly between the buildings as the figure of a man exited the shadows at the end of the block and walked casually down the middle of the street. He carried a small attaché case in his right hand. Molotov didn't move. The footfalls grew louder as the figure neared the alley, stopping only a few feet away. He set the case down. A match flared to life as the man cupped the flame and lit a cigarette. The glow from the flame outlined his small, pockmarked, squinty face and pencil-thin mustache. He wore a white straw Panama hat cocked to one side over his left eye.

Sucking life into the cigarette, he flipped the match away. A sideways glance allowed his beady eyes to make a quick sweep of the plaza across the street. A sarcastic grin appeared at the corner of his mouth as his eyes moved to the alley. He couldn't see Molotov, but he knew the Russian was there. Recovering the case, the Colombian walked the short distance to the alleyway and stepped into the darkness. He still could not see Molotov.

"Mi coronel, I am here."

There was no answer.

"Come now, Colonel, I . . ." The man stepped back,

startled. His cigarette fell from his mouth. It was as if the Russian had stepped directly through the wall and suddenly appeared beside him.

"Ah, puta! You move like the devil," said the frightened man. His voice was unable to conceal the fear that had suddenly shot through him.

"Do we still have a deal?" asked Molotov in a low tone.

"Sí, Coronel. Señor Medina wishes for you to begin the movement of the merchandise as soon as possible."

"And my money?"

The Colombian extended the hand holding the case. "One million dollars as you requested, two million more on arrival of the first shipment, and a final payment of three million when the second shipment has been secured."

Nikolai Molotov reached out to take the case, then hesitated a moment. Once he took the case from this man, he was committed to seeing the thing through. There could be no turning back. He realized that, but there was more at stake than money and reputation. Grasping the handle, he took the case. He was surprised. He had thought a million dollars would weigh more.

"Tell Medina I will initiate the first stage of movement the day after tomorrow. I will expect his agent at the port of Macapá no later than one week from today. If he does not arrive and the authorities discover the true nature of the shipment, that is his problem. I will nevertheless expect to receive my second payment. Señor Medina does understand that, I hope."

Having retrieved his cigarette, the Colombian inhaled deeply. The orange glow from the cigarette was reflected in his black beady eyes. "Sí, mi coronel. You need not worry about such things. I, Rodrigo Arias, am Carlos Medina's agent. I shall be there on time, I assure you. You, señor, must be sure the merchandise is on time and accurate."

Molotov said no more. Turning to walk away, Arias said, "And, Colonel, you will not need to place men into hiding at the port. We are now business partners. Trust should be our motto."

Molotov stopped and turned back to the little man who now nodded toward the plaza across the street.

"You believe I have men watching you, Señor Arias? Did you see them over there or are you just guessing?" asked the Russian officer.

"I have been in this business a long time, señor. I am not guessing. I am certain that you do. How many, may I ask?" said Arias smugly.

Molotov knew there was no possible way that Arias could have spotted his men. He was guessing. Now would be a good time to test the caliber of the men he had reluctantly become involved with. "There are no men over there, Señor Arias. I am here by myself."

Arias hissed under his breath before saying, "You are lying, Colonel."

Molotov smiled in the darkness. His voice was taunting. "There is only one way for you to find out. Why don't you go on over there and see for yourself?"

Arias turned and stared across the street. The moonlight cast an array of shadows over the small park and sent a feeling of nervous uncertainty through the Colombian. The Russian was challenging him, testing him. He began to realize that, but the knowledge did little to change the darkness that enclosed the plaza. Hell with it. He didn't care if there were men hiding over there. Turning back around he said, "I see no need to—" Arias stopped talking. Colonel Nikolai Molotov was gone.

The Buccaneer Club
Tampa Bay, Florida

"Hey, Jake, come on, it's your shot."

Lieutenant Commander Jake Mortimer downed the drink in his glass and asked for another. Leaning over, he gave the gorgeous blonde sitting on the barstool a wet kiss on the ear. At the same time he ran his hand along the inside of her smooth long leg and whispered, "Keep it hot for me, honey, this won't take a minute."

She smiled a knockout smile and nodded as Jake headed for the pool table in the next room. A group of Marines were gathered around the table. Master Sergeant Tommy Smith, the senior crew chief with the Special Operations Wing of SO-COM, was chalking his cue stick and smiling. "They think they've got us this time, Jake."

"That'll be the day!" replied Jake, as he grabbed his stick from against the wall and surveyed the layout of the balls remaining on the table.

Smith and Mortimer had been enjoying a relaxing game of pool when the Marines arrived. In a matter of minutes a challenge was issued and after five straight games, the Marines had not fared well. They hadn't won a single game and were down three hundred dollars. Jake wanted to end it after the second game, but the jarheads didn't want it that way. They kept doubling the bet, and now it all came down to one shot: Jake's shot.

The game was eight ball. Tommy Smith had run off all but one of the striped balls. The Marines had only one solid ball left at the far end of the table and had left the eight ball teetering near the corner pocket on the left end of the table. The ball that Jake needed to make sat precariously close to the eight ball. It would have to be a clean, smooth shot; otherwise, the black ball would drop and the game would be over. The Marines lined along the wall were all smiles as they contemplated how long they could drink on the money they were about to win.

Jake knelt down and studied the angle. Then he walked to the corner and stared straight down at the space that separated the two balls. It was less than a sixteenth of an inch.

"Come on, man, give it up. You know you can't make that shot. Hell, that eight ball's so close to going in that a loud cough will make the damn thing fall," said one of the Marines.

Jake ignored the remark, moved to the other side of the table, and knelt down again to study the angles. Satisfied that he had it figured out, he returned to the far end of the table and leaned forward, positioning the tip of the cue stick within a few inches of the cue ball. Inhaling deeply, he allowed half of the air to ease out as he drew back the stick, smoothly pushing it gently but firmly forward. The click of the tip hitting the white ball sent a wave of dead silence across the room as all eyes locked on the rolling white sphere as it hit the right buffer, smacked into the striped ball, and sent it into the rail and off at an angle for the right side pocket. The solid "cluck" of the ball dropping into the leather basket at the side hole seemed to take the air out of the disbelieving observers who now stared at the unmoved eight ball. The cue ball which had spun backward and curled out to the left, now sat directly in line with the game ball. "Shit!" said one of the Marines.

Jake reached forward, holding the cue stick in one hand, and punched the white ball slightly. It rolled slowly forward and tapped the eight ball, sending it into the corner pocket. Anxious eyes stared at the white ball in the hope that by some magical power they could will the ball to fall into the hole, but it stopped less than a half inch from the pocket.

"Yeah!" yelled Smith as he walked down the line of Marines gleefully pulling money from their outstretched hands. As he reached for the last man's money, the burly Marine buck sergeant held it firmly in his grip, refusing to let it go. "You hustled us, man," said the Marine.

"Oh, come on, Sarge!" said a couple of other Marines. "He made the shot—and it was a hell of a shot at that. He won it fair and square."

"Shut the fuck up. I want anything outta you wimps I'll pull your dicks. This asshole set us up and I ain't gonna let him get away with it," yelled the sergeant, his eyes fired with rage.

Jake tossed the stick on the table and started to walk away. "What's the matter there, boy, you good at shootin' balls, you just don't have any, that right?" jeered the sergeant. A few of the other Marines joined in. "Yeah, tell him, Sarge."

Tommy Smith moved to the other side of the pool table. Folding the money he had collected, he pushed it into his shirt pocket and stared in silence at the sergeant. He would wait to see what Jake was going to do before he said anything.

Mortimer turned around slowly and smiled at the sergeant. "You can keep your money, Sergeant. Remember, we weren't the ones who wanted to keep doubling the stakes, it was you. So, you can keep yours. Buy your boys a few drinks. Matter of fact, Mr. Smith and I will buy the first round. No hard feelings, okay?"

"Fuck off an' die, you Navy shit! We don't need your damn

'good sport' and all that crap. Just have your short little buddy there get up off that money he just tucked away and we'll call it even. Otherwise, we're gonna have to take it back ourselves."

Jake shook his head slowly from side to side and looked over at Smith, who was already rolling up the sleeves of his shirt. The reference to his size had been all he needed. True, Smith wasn't all that big at five-foot-six in stocking feet, but he was built like a brick furnace. Jake had seen the man bench press twice his weight and not even break a sweat. There were seven Marines on the far side of the table. Three of them moved toward the side door. Smith grabbed the pool stick off the table and turned to them. One of them raised his hands. "Whoa, chief! We got no bitch about the game. Your pal won it fair and square as far as we're concerned. We're just going to leave and let you gentlemen discuss the matter. See ya around. Come on, guys, let's get out of here."

Smith turned his attention back to the remainder of the group. "Now, you boys ought to follow those fine upstanding fellows' example and head on out. Otherwise, I'm afraid somebody is going to get hurt."

The sergeant pulled a stick from the rack and broke it over the end of the table. Gripping the improvised billy club tightly in his hand, he started around the table as he yelled, "Ya got that shit right, pop! An' it sure as hell ain't gonna be us. Come on, boys, get 'em."

The room was cleared except for the combatants. Cappy, the owner of the club, stood frozen in the doorway. He looked to Jake for any signal to call the cops, but Jake only grinned and shook his head for the old retired Navy chief to stay out of it.

Smith parried the sergeant's first blow from the club and countered it with an upward swing of the full-length cue stick he was holding. The blow caught the sergeant between the legs, which brought a gush of wind and a scream of pain from the loudmouth who now doubled over and clutched his crotch. Smith pivoted on one foot and brought his knee up with full force, catching the man square under the chin. A sickening crack was heard as the man's jaw snapped. He was sent flying onto the pool table, blood spraying his face.

The second man coming at Smith paused to stare at his shattered leader on the table. It was a mistake. Smith stepped forward, brought his elbow around, and yelled, "You're committed, asshole!" The blow nailed the man on the left side of his chin and sent him sprawling against the wall. Smith moved in and delivered two straight shots to his nose and eye. That was it. The Marine slid down the wall like an overcooked egg on a Teflon pan.

The two men coming at Jake took different routes to get to the Navy commander. One moved around the table, while the other one elected to come across the top. Leaping onto the felt, he made a rush at Jake, who stepped forward and latched onto the man before he could make his jump. Hopping up in the air slightly, Jake hooked one hand under his crotch and with the other, gripped the middle of the Marine's uniform. Utilizing the man's forward momentum, Jake lifted him off the table and sent him flying headfirst into the crossbeam that separated the bar from the game room. The impact made a dull thud as the body came down on top of a group of bystanders.

"Motherfucker!" yelled Jake's second opponent as he clutched a pool ball in his fist and swung it, catching Mortimer below the right ear, stunning him and knocking him back against the wall. Jake's vision blurred for a second. The Marine moved in, raising the ball to bring it crashing down on Jake's skull. The man paused to say, "This is for the sarge, you fuck!" The moment's hesitation was all Jake needed. Sidestepping the downward swing, he brought his clutched fist back in a sudden powerful blow that caught the man on the left cheek. Moving away from the wall, Jake waited until the Marine was on his feet again and turned around before he said, "Game time, jarhead." With that, Jake delivered a staggering shot to the bridge of the Marine's nose. The loud crack of bone breaking resounded around the room and brought a chorus of low mutters from the observers. The Marine dropped liked a poleaxed bull as blood spewed from his shattered and disfigured nose. Jake stepped forward, leaned down, and said, "You talk *after* the fight, asshole."

Smith came around the table. He and Jake went into the bar. Mortimer pulled two one-hundred-dollar bills from his wallet and handed them to Cappy to pay for the damage. Cappy didn't want to take it, but Jake insisted.

Smith pulled the money from his shirt pocket. "Hey, Commander, what about this?"

"You keep it, Smitty. You earned it. Take Nancy out to dinner or something."

"Damn, sir, there's close to five hundred bucks here. You sure?"

"I'm sure, Smitty. Unless my trust fund went bust overnight."

"Oh, yeah, I forget sometimes that you're only in this business for the fun, adventure, and excitement. Hell of a waste of a Harvard law degree, don't you think?"

Jake looked around the bar as he answered, "Naw, not really. Guess I just wasn't cut out to sit on my ass behind a desk and stare out of a thirty-story office through tinted glass."

Turning to the bartender, Jake asked, "Hey, you happen to see what happened to that long-legged blonde that was sitting here earlier?"

"Sure did. She was a real knockout. Left with some young Marines who came out of the game room before the fight started."

Smith laughed so hard that he was about to cry, while Jake ordered a triple Jack Daniel's and Coke. "Oh, well, easy come, easy go," he said.

Smith watched the four Marines being helped out the back door of the club. The hospital wasn't far away. They'd be good as new in a few days. The two Special Ops vets sat at the bar talking about the problems in the Philippines and the release of two American hostages in the Middle East. It was a Friday and both men were off duty. The idea of shooting pool at Cappy's had sounded like a good idea at the time, but now, after the little confrontation with the Marines, Jake and Smitty were content to just sit, talk, and have a few drinks.

Less than an hour had passed when Jake's beeper came to life.

"Shit!" he exclaimed as he slid off the stool, went to the phone at the end of the bar, and called SOCOM Headquarters. After a few minutes, Jake returned to his chair, downed the drink, and tossed some money on the bar. "Come on, Smitty. That was B.J. Something's up back at HQ. He said to bring you along. Maybe we finally drew a mission."

"That's fine with me, Commander. I think the ol' lady's ready for me to take a trip just to get me out from under her feet for a while."

"Well, she's going to get her wish. B.J. didn't say what it was, but he sounded pretty serious over the phone," said Jake.

Finishing his drink, Tommy Smith waved to Cappy as they went out the door, "Later, Cap!"

SOCOM Headquarters
MacDill AFB
Tampa Bay, Florida

Major B. J. Mattson was waiting at the front doors of the headquarters when Smith and Jake drove into the parking lot. Resting his six-foot-four, muscular frame against the wall, he lit a cigarette. Suddenly, he remembered General Sweet's orders about a smoke-free environment. He cupped the cigarette as he glanced quickly up and down the hallway for any sign of the little general with the Napoleonic attitude.

The security NCO at the desk smiled politely. "General Sweet left for the coffee shop a few minutes ago, sir."

Mattson nodded his thanks, lifted the smoke, and drew heavily on the filter. He watched Jake and Smitty joking and laughing as they made their way across the parking lot. They wouldn't be laughing for long. General Raymond Sweet was preparing to tear them both new assholes. There was something about a fight in a civilian establishment, fifty stitches, broken jaws and noses, along with a near skull fracture, and some Marine sergeant who would not be making babies for a while because his testicles were swollen half the size of his head.

B.J. wasn't sure of all the details. All he knew was one minute he was sitting in his office working on an evaluation report and the next thing he knew, General Sweet was storming in, ranting and raving about some call he had received from a Marine Corps general at city hospital who was yelling about a

Navy commander named Mortimer and some SOCOM sergeant, and how they had tried to kill four of his men. The very mention of Mortimer's name was all that was needed to set Sweet off like a bad dynamite charge. B.J. wished General J. J. Johnson, the SOCOM commander, were here. But ol' Q-Tip, as he was known to his men, had taken a well-deserved leave of absence. B.J. had heard that the sixty-year-old general, who had been a widower for over ten years, had met an attractive widow named Helen Cantrell on his last visit to Washington. Mattson didn't want to bother him with something this minor. It wasn't going to be easy, but he'd handle it. General Raymond Sweet was in charge of the unit in Johnson's absence, and B. J. Mattson had been assigned the unpleasant task of serving as the man's adjutant.

B.J. recalled Q-Tip's last words before he left. "B.J., you and Jake stay out of trouble while I'm gone. It's no secret that Sweet would love to nail you two boys to the outhouse door. So walk easy around him until I get back. Don't give him the slightest excuse to fuck with you." It had been a week since those words of wisdom had been spoken, and until now they had somehow managed to steer clear of the acting commander. Jake's little free-for-all had ended any hope of making it two weeks. Sweet now had the excuse he was longing for, a chance to ruin the career of one of SOCOM's top troubleshooters, Lieutenant Commander Jacob Winfield Mortimer IV, Navy SEAL extraordinaire. Bouncing Master Sergeant Tommy Smith out of the Army at the same time was just an added bonus as far as Sweet was concerned. But then, that was the little guy's style.

General Raymond Sweet's dislike for unconventional forces was no secret, although he liked to think it was. Everyone from the private in the mess hall to the secretary of defense knew the man's feelings about SOCOM. Sweet was a conventional infantry officer, and not a very good one at that. He had achieved his status through the combined efforts of certain high-ranking Pentagon officials of the various branches of the armed forces who saw Special Operations Command as a threat to their appropriations war chest. It was hard to justify million-dollar tanks and ten-million-dollar gadgets that didn't work half the time when a six- or twelve-man team of highly trained individuals could get the job done right. Those same officials shared Sweet's dislike of the unit. To them SOCOM was no more than an undisciplined mob of misfits and fuckups who pictured themselves as Rambos out to save the world.

Sweet's job was supposed to have been a simple one: keep an eye on SOCOM's activities and at the first opportunity, use his rank and position to undermine the unit's credibility and usefulness in order to justify disbanding it. So far, Sweet's three previous attempts to accomplish this simple task had ended up embarrassing no one but Sweet and a few of those who had appointed him to the position. Sweet blamed Jake Mortimer and B. J. Mattson for his failures. The only thing that had saved Sweet's job the last time was the fortunate intervention of the Panama invasion. Mattson had to admit that the little general had performed admirably during that campaign. He had wisely informed the Special Operations officers under his command during the invasion to use their own initiative and discretion during the operations. They did, and in so doing, they had made Sweet look good in the press. There seemed to be a bit of irony in that.

Mortimer and Smith came through the doors.

"Yo, B.J., what's going down, man?" asked Jake.

"You and Smitty," said Mattson in all seriousness. "Goddamn it, Jake. The old man warned us to cool it while he was gone. Sweet's after your ass for some damn brawl you two were involved in off post this afternoon. You better come to my office and tell me about it before the little shit gets back here and starts reading you both your rights under Article 32."

Jake and Smitty looked at each other a little dumbfounded. "How in the hell did he find out about that?" asked Jake as they walked down the hall.

"Some Marine general called from the hospital. Said you two should be charged with attempted murder. He must have really torn into Sweet's ass. I haven't seen the little twerp that pissed since the time he got kicked out of Thailand."

Walking into B.J.'s office, Mattson remarked, "My question is, you're both in civvies, so how in the hell did those Marines know your names?"

"You got me, B.J. I guess they could have found out from that blonde I was talking to at the bar before the shit started. She left with some Marines."

Mortimer and Smith sat down in two chairs in front of the desk as B.J. leaned back in his and said, "Okay, let's hear it."

Having explained their side of the story, the two men sat back in silence. B.J. stared down at the top of the polished desk top, slowly turning a pencil end over end in his hand. It seemed to be a clear-cut case of self-defense. The leathernecks had even had a two-to-one advantage and still gotten their butts kicked. But that wasn't going to matter where General Sweet was concerned. He had already ordered that the two men be taken to his office as soon as they arrived.

B.J. let the pencil fall and leaned back. What would old Q-Tip do if he were here? One thing for damn sure, he wouldn't allow Sweet to crucify two of his best people over something like this. Mattson sat quietly searching for an answer to his self-imposed question.

Tommy Smith shifted nervously in his chair and tried to occupy his mind by looking around the office. His eyes came to rest on the three gold-framed certificates on the wall beside him. One was for the award of the Silver Star, presented to Sergeant Robert J. Mattson for "gallantry in action in the Republic of Vietnam." It was dated June 12, 1969. Beside it hung a bachelor of science degree in medicine from Texas A&M, 1974. Below them was a certificate honoring Cadet Commander Mattson as the distinguished graduate of the Texas A&M ROTC program and a copy of the orders commissioning him to the rank of second lieutenant, United States Army. Smith smiled to himself. If there was one person who could get them out of this jam, it was B.J. Any guy who could make it as a Green Beret medic, come out of Vietnam a decorated war hero, face up to the loss of his dreams of becoming a surgeon after having an index finger shot off—and still get a degree and a commission to come right back to this shit, had to be a man you could trust.

Jake was about to say something when B.J. sat upright in his chair and picked up the phone. Punching up the number for an inter-transfer call, he winked at Jake and Smith as he waited for someone to come on the line. It rang twice before a familiar voice answered, "G-2 Intell—Major Tibetts."

"Erin, this is B.J. Look—I've got a situation here that's going to require a set of special orders and immediate departure."

There was a slight chuckle on the other end of the line as Major Tibetts said, "Wondered when you'd be calling, B.J. Those orders wouldn't happen to be for a certain Navy commander and a master sergeant, would they?"

"Shit!" said B.J. "And they swear up and down that this installation is a top-security building. How did you know about this, Erin? Who told you?"

"B.J. I am the Special Ops intelligence officer for Christ sakes. I'm suppose to know what's going on all the time—and I never reveal my sources. When do you want them out of here?"

"We'll need to back-date the departure time. Say, about eight hours," said B.J.

"No problem. We can handle that. Any place in particular you'd like to send these guys?" asked Tibetts.

B.J. paused a moment and stared across the desk at the two men who were leaning forward in their chairs, taking in the one-sided conversation. For a fleeting moment, B.J. had a vision of Jake freezing his butt off in Greenland. He grinned. Mortimer grinned back, his handsomely tanned faced flashing the little dimple that drove all the girls nuts. No, B.J. couldn't do that to his partner. "What have we got open that needs official attention?" he asked.

"Well, let's see. Here's one right up Jake's alley. Coronado, California—the Naval Special Warfare Center. They're testing some new underwater gear and one of those underwater laser prototyes this week. The ol' man will want a detailed report on that one when he comes back off leave."

"That sounds good, Erin. Book Jake for that one. Now, how about Smitty?"

"Hold on a minute, B.J." Mattson could hear the ruffling of papers. Tibetts came back with, "Here we go, B.J. How about Fort Rucker, Alabama? They're having some classes on the new modifications to the Apache assault helicopters. Classes start tomorrow morning. What do you think?"

"Let's go with that. Remember, Erin, back-date the orders and the departure time. You can bet Sweet will be down to check out my story. Can you still forge the ol' man's name?"

"Even he couldn't tell the difference," laughed Tibetts. "I'll have these ready in about thirty minutes. Tell Jake he owes me one. Later, B.J."

Mattson hung up the phone and smiled. "Okay, here's the cover story. That Marine general has the wrong guys. You two weren't even in Florida four hours ago. Jake, you're going out to California—the Naval Special Ops Center. Smitty, you're heading for Fort Rucker. Now get out of here and use the back exits. I don't want Sweet bumping into you. Your orders and travel money will be waiting at the airport. Any questions?"

"This is just like the old days of Special Forces. God, I love it," said Smith as he stood and pumped B.J.'s hand.

"Hell, B.J. If I'd have known I could get a free trip to California, I would have looked up a few Marines a lot earlier," said Jake.

"Don't count on coming out on top with those boys every time, Mr. Mortimer. Believe me, they've got more than a few good men who could clean your clock for you. Now, get out of here and have a good time," said B.J. jokingly.

Both men waved their thanks. Peeking up and down the hall to make sure the coast was clear, they raced across the hall and out the back exit.

B.J. had just sat down behind his desk when the phone rang. It was Sweet. He wanted to know why Mortimer and Smith were not in his office as he had ordered. Mattson informed the general that he was still checking on their whereabouts, but that he would have an answer in a half hour. It was obvious from his tone of voice that Sweet was anything but happy with B.J.'s reply. However, he would accept it for the time being. In thirty minutes, he expected the men to be in his office. If not, he would expect Major Mattson to present himself at that time and explain why he could not find them. Mattson assured the general that he would be in his office on time.

Replacing the receiver, B.J. looked at his watch and

whispered to himself, "Just as soon as I stop by the G-2 orders section, sir." This entire scam was hardly what one would consider action befitting an "officer and a gentleman." However, since Sweet was involved, somehow it just seemed so right.

CHAPTER 2

0800 hours—June 10
Carlos Medina's estate
Mitú, Colombia

Rodrigo Arias swung the white Porsche 924 onto the long straightaway that would take him to the main house of the Medina ranch. White rail fences ran along both sides of the road. There were cattle on the right and herds of horses on the left. It was a huge estate, estimated at close to twenty thousand acres, requiring a staff of over two hundred to care for the main house, the stables, the coffee plantation, and the livestock. Arias had visions of one day ruling over such an empire, but it would take time and patience. He had already achieved one of the major steps in his planned rise to power. Rodrigo Arias was drug lord kingpin Carlos Medina's trusted right-hand man and second in command.

The international outcry against the spread of drugs throughout the world had led to a crackdown on the Colombian drug cartel. Colombia had become a war zone in the battle for control between the dealers and the authorities. Ironically, in terms of firepower, the dealers were better armed than the police or the Army, and had the money to hire entire armies to wage their battles in the streets. For a while it appeared that the cartel would bring the government to its knees, but then the

United States did the unexpected. Working through the United Nations and the world courts, they succeeded in doing what mere guns and explosives could not. Their actions were already taking a toll on the profits derived from the giant cocaine market. However, thanks to Colonel Molotov, Carlos Medina was soon to become the sole ruler of that white powder world. When that was accomplished, Arias would be rewarded handsomely for his contributions to the man's success.

The armed guards atop the ranch house waved to him as Arias stepped from his car to go into the house. Carlos Medina was reading the morning paper and having coffee. Looking up, he folded the paper in half, laid it aside, and stood to greet his old friend. "Ah, Rodrigo, judging from your look, I would guess that all went well at your meeting with our Russian friend."

Arias replied with a smile, "Sí, Carlos, there were no problems."

Medina nodded approvingly and waved to the chair across from him. "Here, sit, Rodrigo. Have some coffee and tell me about it."

Arias watched as the man he had known since childhood poured coffee from a silver container. They were both the same age, forty-three, but from Medina's appearance, one would think he was in his sixties. The once strong, bronzed body had given way to the lure of luxury. Medina was grossly over-weight. His constant eating and beer drinking had added over one hundred extra pounds to his five-foot-ten frame which was intended to carry only a hundred sixty. His cheeks drooped like two overfilled water bags. His face showed the scars of a violent life. His dark brown eyes were tired, not from work, but from the effort it took to lug his heavy body about. Arias promised himself that he would never allow his future wealth to turn him into the grotesque figure of a man that Medina had become.

"So, Rodrigo, tell me what the Russian had to say."

"We talked very little, Carlos. His only concern seemed to be the possible discovery of the merchandise upon its arrival at the port. He told me to remind you that should that happen, it would be our problem, not his."

Medina chuckled. "He is a fool. I have bought and paid for every official in the customs section at the port as well as the governor and mayor of the state in which our new drug lab has been located. I even have the protection of the federal police and the commander of the paramilitary police force in the region. No, Rodrigo, it is not we who should be worried; it is our Russian friend who needs to worry."

A look of seriousness came over Arias as he replied, "I will be honest with you, Carlos, this man does not strike me as the type who worries about much of anything."

"Perhaps that is good. A man of determination seldom fails. Regardless of your opinions, Colonel Molotov is our only hope for achieving total control over the cartel. We must have his merchandise to obtain that goal. His success is our success."

Arias raised his coffee cup in a salute. "To success."

"Success!" cheered Medina as the two china cups chimed together.

0900 hours—June 11
Baroghil Pass
Afghan/USSR border

Nikolai Molotov sat in the shade of the overhanging rocks nestled in the mountainside. His eyes studied the desolate, rock-strewn valley below. Memories of the two long years he had fought in this barren wasteland flashed before his eyes. In his mind he could still hear the echoes of endless artillery and tank barrages. They had proven ineffective against the determined Afghan guerrilla fighters who, in the end, had proven that courage and a strong belief in one's god could overcome destructive technology.

How many Russian lives had this hell on earth claimed before it had ended—twenty thousand, thirty, forty? Who really knew for sure? Even as an intelligence officer, he could not swear to the accuracy of the numbers that were officially given by his own government. Molotov doubted that anyone would ever know the truth.

Afghanistan became Russia's Vietnam. It was a hopeless battle fought only halfheartedly by Afghan government troops which left the Russian soldiers to bear the burden of the fight against a determined enemy. In the end, they, too, had to admit defeat and leave the matter in the hands of those whose fight it had been in the beginning, the Afghan government and the Afghan Army.

Removing a cigarette from the crumpled pack in his shirt pocket, he lit it and watched the smoke curl slowly up and away. An old, familiar sadness came over him. Reaching into his other pocket, Molotov withdrew a weatherworn, cracked photograph. He held it as if it were precious glass as he stared at the young face of the soldier dressed in a Russian officer's uniform. His rank was lieutenant, and his name was Yuri— Yuri Molotov. He was twenty-six years old.

Nikolai's eyes began to mist over as he stared at the picture of his son. Fond memories of his gentle voice and sheepish grin, a trait inherited from his mother, brought a smile to the lips of the weary colonel. The boy's mother was gone now. Pneumonia had claimed her kind and gentle soul some ten years ago. The loss of a woman, a wife, and a friend with whom he had shared nearly four decades of his life would have been more than he could bear had it not been for Yuri. The boy had shown a strength and resolve that had surprised even his father. That strength had helped them both through those first dark and solemn months following her death, and it had bonded together even closer the love of a father for his son.

A sudden breeze of hot, dry air whipped beneath the cliffs and made its way out of the rocks and onto the flat desert of the valley floor below. Molotov watched as the force of the wind, caught in a cross-breeze, began to whirl until three separate dust clouds resembling miniature tornadoes spun wildly for a few feet then dwindled into nothing.

So it had been with Yuri, thought his father. At eighteen, a whirlwind of energy and excitement with his head spinning with talk of military duty, of honor and upholding the Molotov name. Yuri had wanted more than anything to be a soldier like his father, to command the respect and admiration of his country's people, and most of all to make his father proud. Nikolai had tried to delay the inevitable as long as possible; however, it would have been easier to catch one of those dust devils with his bare hands than to hold Yuri back from the military. Finally, after four years of military schools and a commission, Yuri realized his dream. Then came Afghanistan. Nikolai had tried to keep him out of this dreadful place, but to no avail. Only three short months into his tour, Yuri's convoy was ambushed and of the forty-eight-man unit, forty-four bodies had been found. Yuri's was not among them.

Nikolai's search for his son had lasted for two years. Then came the Soviet withdrawal from Afghanistan. There had been a prisoner exchange at the border, but Yuri had not been among those released. The rebels claimed they held no other prisoners. All Molotov's political influence and status as a national hero had achieved little or no response from those in power. Their advice had been simple. The Afghan war was over. It was best for all concerned that he forget it and go on with his life. But how could he? There was no one else. Yuri was his life. For Molotov, the statement had been a paradox comparable to the Americans and Vietnam. The NVA had said there were no more American POWs even though over twenty-five hundred men were still missing. The United States had simply shrugged its shoulders and left its men there to die. The motherland had apparently done likewise. At first Nikolai had refused to believe such a thing. If he could prove that his son was still alive, then surely the motherland would act to ensure his return. Through the use of his vast intelligence network in Afghanistan, he had begun to pass unauthorized messages that promised rewards of money or weapons or both for information about his son. After three long months, his work had paid off. A clandestine meeting had been arranged in Pakistan with the leader of a rebel faction of the Mujahideen. The man had brought the proof the Russian colonel needed, a picture of not only Yuri, but twenty-one other Russian soldiers as well.

It was at this meeting that Molotov was made to realize the awful truth. For almost a year the rebel leader, a man named Abdul Khalig, had been offering to trade all twenty-two men in exchange for arms and ammunition. Russia had refused. This news in itself was bad enough, but not nearly as upsetting as what Khalig had shown him next. The first piece of paper was a message stating that he would execute the prisoners if

Russia did not comply. The reply had been printed on paper that Molotov knew well. It was from the desk of the war ministry. The message contained only three words: "So do it."

From that moment on, Nikolai Molotov vowed to do whatever was necessary to save not only his son, but the other twenty-one prisoners as well. His feelings of bitterness toward the motherland ran deep. The country that he and his only son had served so passionately and without question had turned on them both. So be it, then. There was no longer a feeling of allegiance or commitment to a mother that would abandon her children.

Yanko Voltiski, one of Molotov's trusted Spetsnaz bodyguards, eased around the corner of the rock overhang and said, "They are coming, Colonel."

Carefully folding the picture, Nikolai returned it to his pocket and asked, "They are alone?"

"Yes, Colonel. Mikal has had his glasses on them and radioed from atop the mountain that the two were not being followed."

"Call him and reconfirm that, will you, Yanko?"

"Yes, Colonel." Moving out into the open for better reception, Voltiski removed the small radio from his belt and made the call. The report was the same.

"Good," said Molotov. He grunted slightly when he pulled himself up from the ground. Rubbing at a pain in his back that he knew was no more than old age, he said, "Take your position now, Yanko."

Yanko smiled at the fatherly tone with which the colonel have given the order and departed.

Molotov stretched his aching muscles then bent over and removed a Czech CZ-75 9mm pistol from the case carrying the money. Checking to be sure there was a round in the chamber, he flipped the safety off, brought it around behind his back, and stuck it through his belt with the grip pressing firmly in the middle of his back. Twisting erratically as he jumped up and down a couple of times, he was satisfied that the weapon was securely in place.

Reaching across his chest to the shoulder holster he wore, Molotov removed a second pistol. It was the Beretta model

92F that he had taken from the body of a dead American mercenary in Angola in 1987. Pulling the slide back slightly, he checked the chamber. It was ready to fire. Placing it back in the shoulder holster, Molotov picked up the case and walked out into the open just as the two men he had been waiting for came around the bend at the end of the valley floor. Riding camels, the two wore turbans and the traditional long robes. One carried a rifle slung across his back, while the other had his hanging by the sling from the saddle of his camel.

They were still one hundred yards away when Molotov reached the valley floor. At fifty yards, they halted their camels. As they tapped gently at their animal's legs with their riding sticks, Molotov watched the most reliable transportation in Afghanistan kneel down for the passengers to dismount. Retrieving their rifles and holding them in front of them with outstretched arms, both men hesitated for a moment before laying the weapons on the ground.

Molotov held up both hands to show that he held no weapons. Slowly, he withdrew the Beretta. Holding it high in the air for the two men to see, he placed it on the rocks beside him. Picking up the case, he began walking forward to meet the visitors who were moving toward him. High above them, hidden in the rocks, Yanko tracked the camel riders in the cross hairs of his telescoped sniper rifle. Mikal, his AK-47 leaning on the rocks next to him, continued to scan the terrain surrounding the meeting place with a pair of binoculars. All three of the Soviet soldiers carried the newly developed MX-202 radio. No larger than a cigarette pack, the powerful little radio had a two-mile range. At the first sign of any unexpected guest, Mikal would warn Molotov.

The three met in the center of the valley. The tall man with the beard and one eye was Abdul Khalig. The shorter man was a Pakistani arms dealer. Molotov had not met him before nor did he care to. What Khalig did with the money was of no concern to him, but he had a good idea what the one-eyed rebel had planned. With the Russians gone, it would only be a matter of time before the puppet government that they had left behind would topple like the weak house of cards it had always been. Once the Mujahideen had won the war, there would be a scramble for power among the warring tribes for control of the new government. The one with the most firepower would rule. Abdul Khalig might have only one eye, but he had that eye on the capital city of Kabul and the palace.

Abdul was the first to speak. "Colonel Molotov, I see that you are a man of your word. An exchange in a neutral place with neither side carrying weapons. I am almost certain you have someone watching us at this moment, but I have no problem with that. You Russians have a tendency to trust no one—not even yourselves. May I introduce Mr. Bendri Slalket."

The Pakistani bowed slightly, then reached out his hand, expecting the Russian to shake hands.

Molotov ignored the little man. "Here is your first payment as I agreed. Where are the five prisoners that are to be released?" asked Molotov dryly.

Slalket quickly forgave the affront to his dignity. His eyes were fixed on the case.

Khalig reached into his robe. Molotov tensed suddenly. The cross hairs of Yanko's rifle were resting on the bearded rebel's good eye. If anything remotely resembling a weapon came out from under that robe, Abdul was going to be a blind dead man. Khalig, sensing the mistake of the sudden and unexpected move, quickly and nervously said, "It is only a mirror, Colonel."

"Slowly, please," replied Molotov.

Easing the mirror carefully out of his robe, Abdul stepped back and positioned himself at an angle to the sun. He began to move the glass back and forth. From the side of a mountain less than a mile away, another mirror flashed a reply. Khalig smiled as he started to put the mirror away; then he thought better of it and held it at his side instead.

"Your first five prisoners will be across the Russian border within ten minutes, Colonel Molotov. I, too, am a man of my word."

Molotov removed the radio attached to his belt and pressed the mike switch. "Mikal, can you see them?"

"Yes, Colonel. There are five. They are waving in this direction. Now the Afghan guards are leaving. Our men are walking toward our border, sir."

"I want you to watch them until they are out of sight, Mikal. Call me when they are well into Russian territory and out of harm's way. Out."

Replacing the radio, Molotov glanced down with a sense of disgust as the arms dealer now opened the case on the ground. His dark brown hands pawed over the money like a man caressing a woman.

Molotov looked back to Abdul and asked, "How is my son?"

Abdul's eyes scanned the rocky slopes in a futile effort to locate Mikal's position. Giving it up, he smiled at the Russian as he answered, "He is well, Colonel. He sends his love and anxiously awaits the completion of our transactions in order that you both may be reunited."

The words served to strengthen Molotov's determination to see this thing through to the end. His son was all that remained of his life. His wife was gone; his country had lied to him and betrayed their own soldiers. Now, there was only Yuri.

"When and where shall we meet for the second exchange, Colonel?" asked Abdul.

"One week from today. My agents shall inform you of the place. Ten prisoners for the second payment. Are you certain that none of those being released knows that I am involved in this?"

"I am sure. Only your son knows what you are doing, and as you asked, he has not spoken to the others about your involvement. He is a very obedient son. I have decided that as a show of good faith, I will release twelve men instead of the ten on which we agreed earlier. That will only leave your son and four others to be freed when I receive the final payment. I hope this change in plans meets with your approval, Colonel," said Abdul.

"I assure you, it does."

Molotov's radio came to life as Mikal quietly said, "They are safely across, Colonel."

A feeling of accomplishment revitalized Molotov. Five Russian sons would soon be reunited with their families.

"I would suggest that you two take your money and leave

now. You will receive word when and where our next meeting will be."

Khalig grinned and nodded as he said, "Come, my little friend, I have much shopping to do at your warehouse. Allah go with you, Colonel."

The two turned and walked to their camels. The Pakistani held the money case tightly to his chest. Abdul waved as they rode away, but he only received a long stare from Molotov.

Yanko came down the slope. The sniper rifle was slung over his shoulder. "You have done it, Colonel. Now, perhaps I can convince you to get some rest."

Molotov placed his hand on the young soldier's shoulder. Yanko reminded him so much of his son. "No, Yanko, not yet. But soon, I promise you. Come, we must go now. I want to be in Erfurt, East Germany, by the day after tomorrow. There can be no mistakes with the shipments. Yuri's life and that of the others depend on it."

0800 hours—June 15
USSOCOM HQ
MacDill AFB

B. J. Mattson looked up from his coffee in time to catch a glimpse of a cotton-tufted head as it passed the window next to the entrance of the Officers' Club. A head of hair that white could only belong to one man: Q-Tip, General J. J. Johnson. He had been in Columbus, Georgia, for the last week on leave. General Johnson was not a native of Georgia but said he had always maintained a fondness for the grand old Southern state. B.J., on the other hand, figured the real reason his boss was going to Georgia was to see the attractive and charming widow, Helen Cantrell, whom Johnson had met on his last trip to Washington. She was a senior auditor for the logistics branch at Fort Benning, which also just happened to be the home of the U.S. Army Ranger School. Mattson thought it was a great idea. He hadn't seen the general this happy in a long time. A man of sixty, Johnson's wife had died more than ten years ago. Their only son had been killed in the Grenada invasion a short time later. It was a staggering blow to the old warrior who had seen more than his share of combat in his nearly thirty-year career. No, B.J. would not fault the general for trying to rekindle new meaning into his life.

Johnson spotted Mattson as soon as he came through the door. He waved. B.J. nodded. Two other officers paused to talk with Johnson for a moment. B.J. asked the waitress to bring him another cup of coffee as he looked back at his boss. His camouflage fatigues fit well on his six-foot-two, two-hundred-pound frame. His shoulders were broad, his chest muscular, and his waist trim and neat. For his age, J. J. Johnson was in excellent shape; but then, he was commanding a unit that demanded that each of its personnel maintains above normal physical standards.

Q-Tip was a natural leader. He set the example. His experience was clear in his face. It was a strong face, with weatherworn wrinkles and lines that attested to the hardships of leading men in combat from the bitter cold of Korea to the steaming jungles of Vietnam. Some said the snow-white hair was the result of his countless narrow escapes from death in Vietnam; others said it was brought on the day he received a personal phone call from the president of the United States and was ordered to report to the White House without knowing why. Johnson had been the president's personal choice for the top position in the newly formed United States Special Operations Command. There had been some grumbling from the other branches at first about the ability of an Air Force officer to command a Special Warfare unit, but those criticisms had been silenced after his first year on the job. There was no doubt in Washington or at the Pentagon as to who ran USSOCOM.

Mattson stood as the general approached the table.

Johnson reached out and shook his top troubleshooter's hand as he said, "Sit down, B.J. Good to see you."

"You too, sir," said B.J. "So, how's everything down Georgia way?"

Johnson's eyes seemed to sparkle as he smiled. "Excellent, B.J., absolutely excellent. Colonel Matelan said the young volunteers applying for Ranger School are the best prospects he has seen in years. The same is true of the Airborne School.

Top rate boys, every one. So, tell me, B.J., what's been going on here since I left?"

B.J. shifted to a more comfortable position in his chair. For a moment he thought of asking about Ms. Cantrell, but let it go. His blue eyes stared into those of his boss as he asked, "You mean Sweet hasn't told you about Jake yet?"

Johnson peeked over the top of his uplifted coffee cup. The sparkle in his eyes was still there. "Hell, B.J., I haven't even let that Judas ass know I'm back in town yet. Figured I'd get a factual report from you before having to listen to his bullshit. So tell me. What did our favorite SEAL do to earn the wrath of our resident chicken-shit?"

Mattson briefed the general on the entire incident from beginning to end and finished with, "I figured if you wanted to take a harder line with Jake and Smith on the incident, you could recall them when you got back. I just didn't want Sweet screwing around with them while you were gone."

"You did fine, B.J. I don't see where we have any problems. I'll see the Marine general later today and let him know I am going to take serious action against those who perpetrated the action against those poor innocent boys. I just won't say when I'm going to take that action. What else do we have going on, B.J.?"

Mattson began giving the commander a rundown on the various training and team deployment of the SOCOM personnel, which included an update on the problems in the Philippines. He wrapped the briefing up with a report on an Air Force Civic Action mission that was nearly completed in Brazil.

"Who's in charge of that Civic Action team?" asked Johnson.

Mattson grinned. "Captain Patrica Longly."

Johnson leaned back in his chair. A smile began to form on his lips as he said, "Oh, yes, our commissioned feminist who was so outspoken on women in combat roles at our last staff meeting. How are they doing down there?"

B.J. remembered the staff meeting very clearly. Sweet had made the mistake of characterizing women in combat as "a weak and overly emotional burden that would require fighting men and medics to carry a ton of handkerchiefs for their tears

and a rucksack full of Kotex for their more delicate problems."
The remark had left the men around the table speechless and it
brought a verbal assault on Sweet's own perceived manhood
from the only female present, Captain Patrica Ann Longly, a
1984 graduate of the Air Force Academy and the only female
to ever complete the rugged Air Commando course. She had
particularly noted that Sweet was not wearing jump wings and
was not airborne qualified. Making her point, she extended her
very ample and attractive bosom directly at Sweet to denote the
highly polished silver wings on her chest. Sweet was so
embarrassed that he left the meeting early. The action had
endeared the perky, five-foot-six brunette to every officer
present. When she requested command of the Civic Action
team for the sixty-day Brazilian mission, no one was going to
turn her down.

"They're doing fine, sir. They have ten days left on the
mission. The embassy down there says she's doing a hell of a
job for them," B.J. answered.

Johnson waved for some more coffee before he said, "Good.
Remind me to tell Sweet that, when we go in this morning. I'm
sure it'll make his day."

Both men were laughing as the waitress came to the table
and refilled the coffee cups.

CHAPTER 3

1000 hours—June 15
Tacunica Village
Outskirts of Manaus, Brazil

Captain Patrica Longly removed the needle and quickly swabbed the area with an alcohol-soaked cotton ball while the Jiva Indian boy kept his eyes closed and gritted his teeth tightly together. Removing a cherry lollipop from the stainless steel tray next to the smallpox vaccine bottles, she whispered something in the young boy's ear. His eyes opened and the sight of the candy caused the water that had been welling up in his eyes to suddenly disappear. Nodding his thanks, the boy ran out from under the makeshift medical tent, showed his prize to his mother, and followed her off into the Brazilian jungle.

"How many does that make?" she asked the young Air Force medic sitting at the table across form her where he, too, had just handed out candy to a little girl whom he had vaccinated.

"Eighty-three, Captain," replied Sergeant Johnny Cochran. "I'd say we have about another fifty to go before we can call it a day. Looks like the word is getting around that these gringos aren't so bad."

"I certainly hope so," replied the twenty-seven-year-old

female captain as she pushed a wisp of her black hair back under her jungle hat and prepared another needle.

Sergeant Cochran watched her out of the corner of his eye with admiration and pride. This was the first time he had ever been on a mission with a woman, especially one who was in charge. He, as well as the other three male medics, had had doubts about tracking through the jungles of Brazil with a female, but the spunky little captain had shown them at the very outset that it was not she, but they who were going to have a hard time keeping up with their well-built commander.

Patrica Longly was a native of Florida. She stood five foot six in her stocking feet and weighed a well-proportioned 110 pounds. Her raven hair showcased a smooth, round face with high cheekbones, a button nose, and emerald eyes. Her lips were small, but full and sexy.

Sergeant Cochran tried his best to maintain a professional attitude about the mission and Captain Longly, but after the first three weeks in Brazil he found himself being drawn closer and closer to this woman of strong convictions and compassion. Cochran was not the only member of the team infatuated with the attractive captain. Sergeants Tom Foley and Louis Foster were equally attracted to her. Only Sergeant Odie Watson seem unaffected by the Longly captivation. It had been Watson, a veteran of sixteen years, who had argued against sending a female on this assignment to begin with. He wasn't fooling Cochran who had caught the sarge sneaking a peek at her well-rounded rear end and thirty-six-inch chest that fit ever so well into Captain Longly's tailored jungle fatigues. Watson may not care for female commanders, but even he had to admit she was sure easy to look at.

"Sergeant Cochran," she asked, "can you finish up here? I want to coordinate our next stop with Sergeant Watson."

Cochran felt his stomach twitch as it often did when she spoke his name in that soft, alluring tone.

"Why—yes—yes, Captain, no problem."

She smiled at him, flashing those gorgeous green eyes as she stood.

Cochran watched the smooth rise and fall of her buttocks in

her form-fitting fatigue pants as she walked away. Thank God they only had nine more days out here.

Sergeant Watson was just putting the finishing touches on a bandage he had placed around a young woman's ankle. Motioning to the girl's mother to come near, he said, *"Procar o bandage todo dia."* Having told her to change the bandage every day, he handed the mother a box of gauze. *"Boa sorte."*

The old woman helped her daughter to her feet and they departed.

Watson looked around and saw the captain standing behind him.

"Morning, Captain. How's the shot business today?"

"Fine," she replied as she sat down on a log across from him. "Odie—I mean, Sergeant Watson," Longly quickly corrected herself. She knew what a stickler the veteran NCO was for military protocol, and she was equally aware of his feelings in regard to female commanders. "We have only nine days left before the mission is over; yet in six and a half weeks we have barely covered three percent of the villages that are in need of our help. Sixty days is just not enough time to do all that must be done."

Watson sat back against a tree and lit his pipe. "That's true, Captain. Brazil's a right big stretch of country. We'd need a year in here and still not get all of them. But orders are orders. They said sixty days. You might want to make a suggestion about extending the program in your report when we get back. Other than that, I don't see how we can do much about it."

Longly hesitated as she considered what type of answer she was going to receive from Watson to her next question. She had a feeling it was not going to be favorable. She decided to ask anyway. "Sergeant Watson, do you think SOCOM would consider extending our mission an additional thirty days?"

The crusty old sergeant removed his pipe from his mouth and tapped it on a rock next to him, dumping the smoldering contents in the dirt. Without looking at her, he said, "Yes, Captain, I believe they would." Raising his head, he made eye contact with her. "But I would prefer you not do that."

The answer was what she had expected. "Would you mind telling me why?"

Watson's eyes never diverted from hers as he answered, "Nothing personal, Captain, but if you were a man, it wouldn't be a problem. The way it is, I don't think these boys we have with us can go another thirty days without one of them fucking up. Excuse the expression, please."

"What do you mean, Sergeant, by fucking up?"

"Well, Captain, I figure these boys are already in the early stages of heat from just watching you walk around here in those tight uniforms. Another thirty days of that, and I'm going to have to put a couple of 'em in the stockade when we get back. Don't get me wrong, they're good boys, but I'm afraid it's just a matter of time before one of them decides to step beyond the watchin' and lookin' stage—you know what I mean?"

Longly sat upright as she said, "You can't be serious. Those men are professional military men. The only person who seems to have a problem separating the profession from the gender seems to be you, Sergeant Watson. Well, I think you are way off base on this, and I'm going to make my request to SOCOM as soon as we get back to Manaus." Rising to her feet, the captain walked away.

Watson propped his arms on uplifted knees as he watched her firm ass move smoothly back and forth, straining against her fatigue pants. He called out to her.

She stopped and glanced back at him.

"You asked my opinion, Captain. I gave it to you. Now, you're running this show, so whatever you decide is fine with me. I would suggest, however, that if you are really concerned about the welfare of your troops, that you take a few of those pleated seams out of the ass end of those pants."

Longly turned and looked back at the seat of her pants. Running a hand over the left side, she began to understand what the old sergeant was saying. They were tighter than she realized. "Thank you, Sergeant Watson. I may do that this evening. Would you please plot our next movement and write up the request for the additional medical supplies we will need?"

Watson tipped his jungle hat. "My pleasure, Captain."

She smiled, then turned and walked away. Watson removed

his map from the side cargo pocket of his fatigues. He liked the
lady. She had confidence in herself. If he were ten years
younger he, too, would be having the same wet dreams these
kids were having about balling the captain; but he was past that
stage now. Spreading out the map, he marked the next stop for
the Civic Action team, a place called Santo Antoñio do Içã.
They would arrive there in two days.

1100 hours—June 15
Erfurt, East Germany

Yanko Voltiski remained outside with the car while Molotov
and Mikal went inside the plant. They went directly to the
office of the manager, Herr Rudolf Schmidt.

The gray-haired man in his late sixties stood as the two
Russians came through the door. "Ah, Herr Rubens, so good
to see you again."

Rubens was the cover name Molotov was using for this part
of the operation. Schmidt was sure that the name was an alias,
but business was business and Herr Rubens was paying in
cash. Therefore, he could call himself any name he pleased.

Mikal placed a briefcase on Schmidt's desk and stepped
back.

The man opened it and smiled. Inside was another payment
of twenty-five thousand dollars. This money was part of the
original advance that Molotov had extracted from Medina at
their first meeting. Another two payments of twenty-five
thousand dollars each were to be paid to Schmidt following
each shipment.

Molotov sat in a chair near the door and said, "I hope that
all is going well from your end, Herr Schmidt."

Closing the case and sliding it under his desk, the plant
manager smiled broadly as he replied, "Exactly as planned and
on schedule, sir. All of the merchandise has been relabeled and
your first shipment of twenty-six hundred barrels will arrive at
the port in Brazil on the sixteenth. That is tomorrow, probably
in the afternoon. Your second shipment has already cleared the
West German port and is en route. It will arrive on the
nineteenth, again in the afternoon. The third and final shipment

is being prepared at my warehouse even as we speak and will be transported across the border and to the West German port within the next seventy-two hours. As I stated, Herr Rubens, the Schmidt and Sons Company is a very efficient organization."

Molotov stood and opened the door to leave. Looking back at the German black marketer, he said, "I certainly hope so. Many lives depend on those shipments arriving where and when they are supposed to. Yours included, Herr Schmidt. Good day."

Schmidt seated himself behind his desk and pulled out the money once more. At the same time he considered Rubens's last remark. Picking up the phone, he dialed the number for the warehouse and instructed his foreman to add another twenty workers to the loading and securing of the barrels. He wanted them out of the warehouse and on their way in the next forty-eight hours. This would be the third and final shipment. The sooner he was rid of it, the better.

1300 hours—June 16
Port of Macapá, Brazil

Rodrigo Arias watched the unloading of the cargo from the hold of the huge ship flying the Danish flag. Molotov and Yanko stood beside him as the first pallets were lowered to the dock. Arias waited until the net had been removed before going to the nearest barrel. Using his knife, he pried open the small cap at the top of the fifty-five-gallon drum and bent forward. Sniffing once, he brought his head back up abruptly and secured the cap back in place. Turning to one of Medina's men, he instructed him to remain on the dock and to count each and every barrel marked "Lubricating Oil." He was to bring the total count to the restaurant located at the end of the docks when he was finished. The man began his work.

Arias smiled at the two Russians. "Come. We can get out of the sun and have a bite to eat and enjoy a cold *cerveza* while we wait."

Molotov nodded toward the three customs men approaching the ship.

Arias assured him that they had already been taken care of. They would inspect all the cargo except the barrels. He showed Molotov a stamp at the corner of each of the pallets. "They were cleared while they were still in the hold, my friend. You worry too much, Colonel. We know what we are doing, believe me."

"As you say." Molotov shrugged. "A cold beer does seem good. Shall we go?"

Arias led the way to the restaurant. Once inside, they all ordered beer. Yanko sat with his chair sideways to the table. The buttons of his lightweight jacket were undone in order to allow quick access to the Beretta strapped in the shoulder holster beneath his right armpit.

Arias downed half his beer in one long gulp before nodding toward Yanko. Joking, he said, "You Russians are not very trusting, are you, Colonel?"

"It depends on who we are dealing with, Señor Arias. Some we trust more than others," replied Molotov.

"You have no worry here. You see those eight men sitting at the bar and the other four near the door? Those are my men. I run a smooth operation, Colonel. Perhaps, after we have done business for a while, you will begin to feel more at ease with the situation. I hope so. I am going to need you more and more as my business grows."

Molotov took note of the reference to "my business."

"Excuse me, Señor Arias, but I was under the impression that this was Señor Medina's operation, not yours. Or has there been a change in power since I have been gone?" asked Molotov, rather loudly.

Arias looked around at his men, who had turned toward the table. His voice was nervous. "No, no, Colonel, you misunderstood what I said. It has always been Carlos Medina's business, and so it shall always be. I am but a simple servant."

The men around the room returned to their discussions as Arias pulled a handkerchief from his jacket and wiped the sweat from his brow.

"You must watch what you say, Colonel. There are many ears in this country and such talk can have very bad repercussions for those who speak out of hand."

Molotov smiled, as did Yanko, who said, "Yet you speak to us of trust, Señor Arias. I find that very interesting."

Arias didn't say any more. The next hour was spent in relative silence as the three ate and drank. By the time they had finished, the man from the docks came in and handed Arias a slip of paper with the number of barrels tallied from the shipment. It was exactly twenty-six hundred barrels. Arias ordered the trucks loaded for immediate departure. Signaling to a man at the bar to join them, Arias stood up and said, "Your numbers are exact, Colonel. I must go now, but I will be here the day after tomorrow for the second shipment." The man from the bar placed a large case on the table in front of Molotov.

"Here is your money as agreed," said Arias. "I shall see you soon, Colonel. Adios, amigo."

The cantina emptied except for a peasant in the far corner of the room who appeared to have passed out. His sombrero covered his face. Molotov waited until Arias and his men had departed before opening the case. The money was all there. Locking the case again, Molotov called out to Mikal. The young Spetsnaz officer pushed his sombrero back and slid the Uzi submachine gun back under his serape before he left the corner table to join Molotov.

Placing the case in Mikal's hands, Molotov whispered, "Here is the money, Mikal. You must leave for Afghanistan today. Tell Abdul Khalig that I had to stay here in order to secure the final payment, but that I will be there with the rest of his money when my son is released—and Mikal, be careful. I believe Khalig can be trusted, but I am not as sure of his Pakistani friend. You must make them think that you have other men hiding in the rocks. If they believe there is a rifle pointed at their heads, I think they will disregard any ideas of betrayal. Now, go, my friend."

Mikal shook hands with his two friends before leaving. He would be in Afghanistan by tomorrow morning. Molotov leaned back in his chair and sipped at his beer. The colonel had tried to maintain a totally professional attitude about this business. He tried not to become overanxious or allow his hopes to get out of control, but it had not been an easy task. As he watched Mikal go through the door, he felt a sense of achievement. His son was one day closer to freedom.

2100 hours—June 16
Officers' Club
MacDill AFB, Tampa Bay

General Johnson sipped at his martini, laughed, and tipped his glass to Major Mattson. "Yes, sir, B.J., General Sweet is convinced that you did something illegal by getting Jake and Smitty out of here as fast as you did. Those orders with my signature had him stumped. He must have asked me five times if I remembered signing them before I left. Which reminds me, I'll have to speak to Major Tibbets about that. I'd like to know how he got so good at signing my name."

B.J. removed the olive from his drink and laughed with the general. He was about to bite the olive off the stick when he saw General Sweet and his wife enter the dining room. "Well, speak of the devil," said B.J., nodding toward the entrance.

Johnson shifted in his seat to look over his shoulder. "Let's just hope he doesn't want to join us," said Johnson.

Sweet surveyed the room and spotted Mattson and the general. Sending his wife to their reserved table by herself, he walked toward B.J. and Johnson.

"Here he comes," said Mattson.

Sweet ignored B.J. as he stepped to the table and said, "Ah, General Johnson. Glad I ran into you. I was just at the office. We have received a request from that Captain Longly woman to extend the Civic Action mission in Brazil for another thirty days. Personally, I don't think we should."

Mattson sat back and tried not to bite his martini glass. Sweet's voice had an irritating, high-pitched squeak that set B.J.'s teeth on edge. If they had been sitting in a club in Hollywood in the forties, everyone in the place would have thought that Peter Lorre had walked up to their table. Sweet had the same round little body and squinty face that nearly concealed his beady little eyes. His few strands of hair were layered to one side to cover a large bald spot. Try as he might, B.J. could not force himself to like anything about this man.

"Well, thank you, Raymond. I'll take your opinion under advisement and make my decision in the morning," replied Johnson.

"Very well, sir. Enjoy your dinner, sir," said Sweet as he left to return to his table.

Mattson placed his glass on the table. "It would appear that I am still on the fat man's shit list. You notice he didn't say hello, good-bye, go fuck yourself, or anything."

"Did you want him to?" asked Johnson.

"Naw, guess you're right. Better leave well enough alone. So, tell me, sir, how is Ms. Cantrell doing down Georgia way?"

The general pulled one of his favorite cigars from the inside pocket of his dinner jacket and lit it.

One of the waiters hastily appeared at the table. His tone was apologetic as he said, "I am sorry, sir, but there is no smoking in the club."

Johnson kept puffing until there was a bright red glow at the end of his cigar. Lowering it, he looked up at the waiter. "Is that right?" he asked. "And just whose dumb-ass idea was that?"

The waiter became uncomfortable as the people around them stopped eating and stared at him. "It was ordered by the post commander, General Hastings himself, sir. Over a week ago."

Johnson let a long trail of smoke make its way across the table as he said, "Well, that's okay then. It doesn't apply to me. You see, garçon, I'm a fucking general, too. Now, go squeeze your lobster tails or whatever it is you do and let me enjoy myself."

The waiter's face flushed as he bowed before he left.

The tables were alive with hushed whispers. "It's no wonder that unit is such a rowdy bunch if that's an example of their leadership.

Johnson didn't care what they thought. If he wanted to enjoy his after-dinner cigar, he was going to.

"Helen is doing fine, B.J.," said Johnson in answer to Mattson's earlier question. "She had to go on an unexpected audit to Fort Sill, out in Oklahoma. That's down around your neck of the woods, isn't it, son?"

"Yes, sir, it is."

"So, tell me, how are you and Charlotte doing these days?"

Now it was Mattson who was uncomfortable. "Oh, we're still talking things over, sir. She and the kids are staying with her folks. She keeps wanting me to get out of the Army, and I keep saying I will, but I'm just not ready yet. Being apart like this gives us both time to sort it all out. At least there hasn't been any talk of divorce over it."

Johnson hated the thought of losing one of his best men. However, he was equally disturbed about what was happening to this fine officer's family. He couldn't count the times his wife had left him over the thirty years they had been married. He was sure that most men who had been in the military more than ten years had experienced the same problem at one time or another.

"Listen, B.J., like I say, Helen is going to be in Okalahoma for about a week. If you think it might help, I could see if she could stop by and speak to Charlotte about it. Helen's been around the military almost as long as I have. What d'you think?" asked Johnson.

B.J. smiled. "Hell, General, it couldn't hurt. Thank you, sir. I appreciate it."

"No problem, son. I'll call Helen tonight. Now, do you think that waiter's too pissed off to bring me an ashtray?"

B.J. grinned. "Well, sir, he just might be. Looks like you started something here."

Both men looked around the room. People at nearly every other table were smoking. Across the room, General Sweet had the waiter by the arm and was pointing wildly to a sign that stated in big red letters, "No Smoking."

CHAPTER 4

Molotov and Yanko sat at a corner table in the same restaurant that Arias had brought them to during the first exchange. Mikal had returned from Afghanistan, arriving in the port city only an hour ago. Molotov listened intently as the young Russian officer detailed the events of the second POW exchange.

Abdul Khalig had arrived with the Pakistani as before. The Afghan leader had seemed disappointed that Molotov was not present to greet him, but he understood. Enlisting the help of two other Spetsnaz officers loyal to Molotov, Mikal had utilized one for security in the rocks, while the other was hidden a few hundred yards from the release point along the Russian border. The Pakistani had inspected the money while Abdul signaled his men in the mountains for the release of the prisoners. True to his word, the rebel leader had released twelve men. Following Molotov's instructions, Mikal had informed Abdul that the third and final payment would be forthcoming in seven days. The Afghan seemed pleased with the arrangement and wished the colonel well in his venture. Then he rode away with the money.

Finishing his story, Mikal looked across at Colonel Molotov. His eyes gleamed with admiration as he said, "Our brothers in the Spetsnaz who helped me said that the news of the return of the first five prisoners gained national attention in the world press and that the interviews conducted with them and their families were shown hourly on national television."

A worried look wrinkled Molotov's brow.

"Do not worry, my colonel. They have no idea that you are involved in their release. Abdul Khalig has graciously taken credit for that. He has cited the teachings of Allah, which state that one should take pity on a defeated enemy. In a personal interview with American reporters, he vowed to release all of his prisoners within a week's time. I would imagine the freeing of the twelve yesterday has caused quite a stir among the international media again today."

Molotov couldn't help but grin as he said, "That is one smart son of a bitch. With the money we have provided him, he can buy enough firepower and political backing to establish himself as the new leader of Afghanistan, and all with the approval of a world that sees him as a great humanitarian and true practitioner of his faith. Yes, indeed, Khalig is a very smart man."

A round of laughter broke out at the bar where Rodrigo Arias and his small army of bodyguards whiled away the time tormenting the strikingly beautiful young waitress as she went in and out of the kitchen, having to pass the group each time she did so. One of them slapped her on the butt as she disappeared into the kitchen once more. The Russians watched as Arias huddled his men around him for a moment. He said something to them which brought a murmur of laughter from the men. Then he stepped back against the bar to wait for the girl to come out again.

The swinging door opened and she exited with a tray loaded down with glasses of water and dinner plates. One of the men reached out suddenly and grabbed her around the waist, sending the tray crashing to the floor. The two couples for whom the dinner had been intended quickly rose and left the restaurant. Another of the men stepped forward and pulled the elastic band at the top of the girl's colorful blouse down around her waist, exposing her small but firm young breasts. She screamed.

The restaurant owner, an elderly man, rushed out of the kitchen. Seeing what was happening, he turned to Arias, told him that the girl was his daughter, and asked that he have her released. The grin on the Colombian's face quickly disappeared. It was replaced by a look of pure arrogance and evil. Arias came off the barstool like a shot. Grabbing the old man by the front of his shirt, he pulled the man to him and spat in his face. Laughing, he told his men to strip the girl.

Yanko reached inside his jacket to grasp his 9mm automatic resting in his shoulder holster. Molotov grabbed his arm and stopped him from drawing the weapon.

Two of Arias's men moved to the front of the restaurant. Closing and locking the doors, they returned to the bar to watch the fun. The girl screamed again as rough, grabbing hands tore her clothes from her body. The old man fell to his knees at Arias's feet and begged for his daughter to be set free. She was only fifteen and still a virgin. That news only served to excite the Colombian even more. Placing his foot on the old man's chest, he pushed him over and onto the floor.

Yanko, his hand still gripping the gun inside his coat, pleaded with his eyes for Molotov to do something, anything, to stop this. Mikal's hand disappeared inside his jacket as well, signifying that Molotov need only give the word and they would stop the deplorable act. Molotov shook his head no. Yanko and Mikal were both young men. They had only been involved in a few limited combat engagements and had not seen the cruelty and atrocities of the real world as Molotov had. He, too, wished that he could stop this, but as he had taught at the Spetsnaz school, logic must always overrule emotion. Yanko and Mikal had obviously forgotten that lesson. There was more at stake here than a girl's virginity. Freedom for his son and four of their comrades depended upon what they did in the next few seconds. Besides, Arias had eight men with him, all armed, most with automatic machine guns. The restaurant was a very small place to start a war, especially when outnumbered three to one.

"Please, Colonel," begged Yanko, as the men threw the girl onto her back on the table. Molotov again shook his head no. One of them pulled her arms back and held them outstretched behind her head. Two others grabbed her ankles and slowly pulled her legs apart. Sobbing, she pleaded with the men to let her go. They laughed as the tears streamed down her cheeks.

Arias grabbed a bottle of whiskey that was sitting on the bar. Staring over at Molotov with a sadistic grin, he turned it up to his lips and gulped down three large swallows of the liquor, draining nearly a third of the contents. Slamming the bottle back on the bar, he wiped his mouth with the back of his hand and moved toward the girl. His eyes were dancing wildly in anticipation as he began to unbuckle his belt. His men cheered him on as they held the struggling little body tightly drawn across the table.

"Colonel, can we do nothing?" whispered Mikal, who had removed his hand from his gun and now sat with his hands balled into tight fists on top of the table. Yanko could tell by the colonel's eyes that his mind was searching for an answer or an idea, some way to help this girl.

"What time is it, Yanko?" asked Molotov calmly.

"It is 12:30, Colonel."

"Good. The man Arias placed on the dock to watch the unloading is supposed to come for him when the first barrels are brought out of the cargo hold. Arias must be there to make sure that the customs people ignore the merchandise once the unloading begins. That should begin very soon. I want you both to remain at the table. I am going to attempt to stall for time. If things should get out of hand and weapons are drawn, protect yourselves and get out of here as quickly as you can. Do not worry about me. Do you both understand?"

Both men nodded that they would obey.

Molotov stood and walked toward the bar. Arias, ready to drop his pants and step between the girl's outspread legs, now hesitated as he watched the big Russian approach.

"So," laughed Arias, "you like to watch, huh, Colonel? As my guest, I would offer you first go at this young bitch. But at your age, I fear she would still be a virgin when you finished."

The remark brought a howl from the bodyguards.

Molotov only smiled as he stepped forward and stared down at the frightened girl. Her tear-filled eyes were darting from side to side like a terrified animal caught in a trap. It was a look Molotov had seen more times than he cared to remember.

Turning to Arias, who now stood with his legs slightly apart to hold up his pants, he said, "So, you think this Russian is too old to deflower this young tigress, do you, Mr. Arias? Well, I shall make you a wager, my friend. The winner shall have the honor of introducing our tender little virgin here to womanhood. What do you say, sport?"

The room was silent. All eyes were on Arias. The girl's father had managed to pull himself up into a sitting position against the wall, praying silently for his only child.

A smirk was on Arias's face as he said, "You cannot be serious, Colonel. What challenge could a man of your years propose that I could not easily win?"

"We shall drink for her!"

"What?"

"Drink, Mr. Arias. The same way you demonstrated your abilities only a few moments ago with that bottle at the bar. Or is your sexual prowess with women the same as your drinking—three quick shots and you're finished!"

Arias's men broke out in another round of laughter at the colonel's remark. A threatening glare from their leader quickly silenced the group. Molotov stood between Arias and the girl with his feet apart and his hands on his hips, awaiting the man's reply to his challenge.

Pulling his pants back up, the Colombian jerked his belt back into place and stomped off behind the bar. Grabbing four bottles of whiskey from under the counter, he placed them on the bar and shouted, "Come on, you old fool. Even drunk I can service that young whore better than you."

Molotov glanced down at the girl once more and winked, giving her a kindly smile. The fatherly look she saw in his eyes helped ease her terror. She sensed that this man meant her no harm.

One of the men brought forth a tray of whiskey glasses and set them on the bar. Arias poured two glasses full and set one in front of Molotov, saying, "When we have finished off a glass we will line them up in front of us. It will be easier to count that way. Agreed?"

The colonel didn't bother to answer. Picking up the glass, he tossed it down in one gulp and placed the glass in front of him. The contest was on.

Twenty minutes and twelve shot glasses later, the two adversaries stared at each other across the short distance of the bar that separated them. Arias's eyes were glazed and watery. Molotov knew the man could not last much longer.

Arias looked over at the naked girl who was still being held on the table by two of his men. The sight excited him. Pushing his glass away, he mumbled, "Hell with this game. I want to fuck the bitch."

Molotov's eyes glanced at the clock. Ten more minutes; that was all he needed. Arias started to move along the bar, heading for the girl. Molotov quickly grabbed his glass, purposely let it fall from his hand, and staggered against the bar, grabbing the edge as if trying to steady himself; Arias stopped. The old man was about to go down. The eyes of his men were on him. He could not let this old man defeat him in this challenge. The girl could wait a few more minutes. Returning to stand in front of Molotov, Arias poured two more glasses of whiskey. "Come, Colonel, doooo—not quit on me—yet." Arias's words were becoming slurred and he was rocking slightly. The bodyguards sensed victory at hand for their leader and began to cheer him on. Molotov made an exaggerated effort to steady himself. He slowly, feebly raised his glass to his lips and drank. Arias poured again.

Yanko and Mikal rose from their seats and started toward the bar.

Yanko moved next to the man holding the girl's arms. The man was short and was standing on his tiptoes to watch the action at the bar. "Go ahead, my friend. You cannot see from here. I will hold the girl for you," said Yanko as he carefully pushed the man's hands away and replaced them with his own.

The bodyguard paused a moment, unsure of what he should do, then shrugged his shoulders and joined the others at the bar.

The man holding her feet looked at Yanko and asked, "Can you hold her by yourself, señor?"

"No problem, go ahead," said Yanko, smiling innocently.

Molotov lowered another glass from his lips. Out of the corner of his eye he was well aware of what the two young Russian officers were doing.

Mikal slowly helped the old man to his feet. Moving quietly and with purpose, he maneuvered the old man along the wall and over to his daughter's side.

Yanko had her sitting up. She clung to the shredded clothes that he had recovered from the floor for her, in a futile attempt to cover her nakedness.

Her father now stood only a few feet away. He started to go to her, but Mikal held him back and shook his head, whispering, "No, señor, not yet. I will tell you when."

Arias's aim with the bottle was becoming worse with each drink. His attempts to refill the glasses led to half the bottle running out across the bar. But he was now determined to outlast this old man who seemed on the verge of collapse. Only a few more drinks, and he would have him. Molotov's shaking hand brought the glass up to his lips as he stared over the top of the drink at the clock on the wall that showed one o'clock.

The colonel could tell by Arias's eyes that the man was on the verge of passing out. The glass teetered precariously at the Colombian's lips as he tried to force his mouth open. Leaning his head back, Arias lost his balance, fell into the stacks of bottles and glasses behind him, and slid to the floor behind the bar.

Two of his men ran around to help him to his feet, while the others leaned óver the bar to watch. Molotov quickly looked to Yanko and nodded toward the side door. Within seconds, the old man and girl were out the door and down the alley. Yanko and Mikal joined Molotov at the bar.

Arias was babbling incoherently and trying to pull his arms free from the two men who were the only stabilizing force holding him up.

Someone knocked on the locked front doors. One of the bodyguards went to the curtain and peeked out to see who it was. He turned to the group, his face pale. "Damn! It is *el jefe*—Medina is here."

There was a wild scurry of activity as Arias was pulled around from behind the bar and placed in a chair at one of the tables. The bodyguards positioned themselves around the room.

Molotov and his group remained at the bar. There was another banging on the door, more forceful this time. The man at the door pushed the bolt free and opened it wide for the drug lord.

Medina's bodyguards came in first. Making a quick check of the area, they signaled to their boss that it was all clear.

Large sweat stains were already spreading from the fat man's armpits, down the sides of his colorful lavender shirt with the pea green flowers and an ugly yellow rose over the pocket. It was all Yanko and Mikal could do to keep from laughing at the spectacle.

Molotov recognized the man behind Medina. He was the pickup man for the money to be paid, the customs officials on the dock. Beside him stood the lookout who was to have informed Arias when the barrels were unloaded. None of the men in the doorway appeared in a good mood.

Medina made his way across the room, his rows of fat causing the shirt to wiggle and bounce like a colorful bowl of Jell-O. He stopped in front of the table where Arias sat, barely able to lift his head. Using the end of a thick teakwood cane that he carried, Medina placed one end under Arias's chin and forced the man's head back.

"Bastardo!" yelled Medina. "You sit on your ass and get drunk while my shipment is being placed on the docks under the watchful eye of officials who have not been paid their money."

Arias tried to talk, but his whiskey-sodden brain could not think nor his thick tongue find the words.

"Shut up! You son of a donkey's ass. I should have your fucking brains blown out here and now."

One of his bodyguards stepped forward quickly with a .357 magnum in his hand. He pointed the weapon less than an inch from the back of Arias's head. No one spoke. Molotov stood with his foot on the bar rail sipping at his whiskey, waiting with cold curiosity for the fat man's decision.

Medina removed the cane and waved the gunman away. Shouting orders for the man to get Arias to the car and for the rest of them to get to the docks and help with the unloading, Medina waved the lookout over as he thrust a wad of money in his hand and instructed him to see that the customs people were paid.

Only Medina and three of his men remained in the room with Molotov, Mikal, and Yanko. Plopping his huge buttocks on one of the barstools, Medina poured himself a drink and said, "I am sorry for the inconvenience, Colonel. I don't know what got into Arias. He is normally my most dependable man." Noting the long row of whiskey glasses in front of Molotov, he raised his glass and remarked, "You must like our whiskey, Colonel Molotov."

The Russian's eyes were clear and alert as he poured himself another drink. "It is all right, I suppose. As a young man, I was raised in the Ukraine. We often made our own to ward off the bitter cold of the north winds. I became rather fond of it, but it was much stronger than this." Molotov downed his glass, then asked, "Shall we go inspect the cargo?"

"It has already been done. There is no problem, Colonel. It is as good as the first shipment. I had no doubt that it would be," replied Medina with a smile.

"Then may I have my money, please?"

Medina placed his glass on the bar and turned to face Molotov. "But of course, uh—uh—Nikolai, isn't it? Would you mind if I addressed you by your first name?"

"As you wish," said Molotov.

"Good. Nikolai, I have a proposition for you. As I am already embarrassed by Arias's unprofessional behavior in this matter, I would consider it an honor if you and your men would return with me to my hacienda. The final shipment is not due for five days. You could enjoy the leisure of my estate. We have fine food, plenty of whiskey—or vodka, if you prefer— more luscious women than you will find in this pesthole of a city, and two swimming pools for your enjoyment. It would give us a chance to discuss business. What do you say, Colonel?"

Molotov hadn't planned on this. He was not a man who liked changes once an operation had begun. "I'm sorry, Mr. Medina, but it is vital to my other plans that the money from this shipment leave the country this afternoon."

Medina paused a moment, a look of disappointment clearly visible on his face. Turning the glass in slow circles on the bar, and deep in thought, Medina looked up again, the smile returning to his chubby-cheeked face. "Okay, Colonel, since the financial portions of this deal are of obvious importance to you, I shall offer another proposal. You agree to visit with me at my hacienda, and I in return will pay you not only the money due from this merchandise, but the money for the final shipment as well. You see, Colonel, that is how much confidence I have in you."

Molotov felt a surge of excitement shoot through him like a lightning bolt. Yuri and the other four prisoners could be free by tomorrow evening. The realization that all of his work and hopes now lay within his grasp nearly took his breath away. He could be with his son in a matter of days. Fighting to control the emotions of joy that filled him, Molotov said, "I am honored that you show such trust in me, Señor Medina; however, if I should accept your gracious invitation, it would still be necessary for one of my men to depart with the money tonight in order to meet my other obligations."

"That is perfectly acceptable, Colonel. My private plane is at the Manaus airport. We can be at the ranch in one hour. I shall turn over the money to your man and my pilot will fly him wherever he wishes to go. Then we have a deal, Colonel?" asked the drug lord.

Molotov nodded and said, "We do, Señor Medina. When would you like to leave?"

"Right now will be fine. My plane has air-conditioning. This insufferable heat is very hard on me. Shall we go?"

Molotov waved his hand toward the door. Medina and his men went out first. As they departed the restaurant, Molotov placed a small stack of banded money, which had fallen from Arias's pocket, next to the register in payment for the damage they had caused and the trauma suffered by the young girl and her father. The number on the brown wrapper read "$5,000.00."

• • •

By five o'clock in the afternoon, Molotov was giving Mikal his instructions for his final meeting with Abdul Khalig. Medina's pilot had already refueled the twin-engine Beech aircraft that had brought them to the estate along the Colombian border, only three miles from Brazil. Two suitcases loaded with money were placed in the plane as they talked. Mikal was to phone Molotov at the estate as soon as possible after the exchange. Farewells were exchanged, and the young Russian officer climbed into the plane. He waved to Yanko and Molotov from the copilot's seat as the twin-engine aircraft shot past them, lifted skyward, and disappeared over the mountains. Everything was going as planned. The only alteration to the plan was the surprise decision by Medina to pay the entire amount on this trip, but that had been a welcome surprise. As the colonel and his friend Yanko walked back toward the ranch, Molotov's confidence was higher than it had been since the long operation had begun. He had covered all the bases like any good Soviet intelligence officer should—all but one: the one that has plagued great men and great ideas since the beginning of time, the always-present threat of what has become known as Murphy's Law, which says that if anything can go wrong, it will.

The famed axiom was about to rear its ugly head to intervene in the flawless plan of Colonel Nikolai Molotov.

0800 hours—June 20
Erfurt, East Germany

Herr Rudolf Schmidt was humming to himself as he pulled up to the front gates of the Schmidt and Sons pharmaceutical plant. It was going to be a beautiful day, and the man was in great spirits. The last order for Herr Rubens's shipment had been moved to the docks at Esbjerg, Denmark, and loaded aboard a ship that had departed on the nineteenth. That meant another twenty-five thousand dollars profit for the well-to-do black marketer. Add to that the sizable amount he was to receive today from a far-right radical group calling itself the Islamic Path, who had requested a special blend of chemicals that he had manufactured, and all told, it had been a very profitable week, indeed.

Recognizing the car as it pulled up to the gate, the security man inside pressed the electronic button that disengaged the bolt and swung the gates open. Schmidt stopped next to the man and inquired as to any early arrivals this morning. The guard informed him that a van carrying four Arabs had arrived less than thirty minutes ago. Schmidt smiled and thanked the man as he drove to his parking space in front of the building. He was still humming to himself and there was a noticeable spring to his step as he nodded politely to the receptionist and went into his office. Pressing the button on his intercom, Schmidt asked if his son had arrived for work yet. He had not, but there was an Arab gentleman waiting to see him. Schmidt told the girl to have him come in.

The tall, dark-skinned man called himself Mohammad, and he carried a briefcase with him which he placed on the table next to Schmidt's desk.

"We are here to finalize our agreement," said the Arab in a rather low and suspicious tone.

Schmidt walked around his desk and opened the case. It was all there, fifty thousand dollars in American bills.

"Authorization for the release of your shipment shall be sent at once, Herr Mohammad. I hope tha—" The sudden sound of gunfire in the building interrupted Schmidt before he could finish.

Mohammad jerked open the door just as another Arab carrying a submachine gun burst into the outer office. Blood was spreading down the left sleeve of his shirt. The receptionist screamed and leaped to her feet. The bleeding man never hesitated. Bringing the machine gun up, he fired a short burst that slammed the startled woman back against wall. Four bullets ripped through her body and splattered her blood on the wall and ceiling.

Schmidt stood as if paralyzed, trying desperately to comprehend what was happening.

The two Arabs exchanged words quickly and the man called Mohammad turned on Schmidt. His eyes were wild, the gaze of a man who felt he had been betrayed. Slowly pulling a pistol from his inside coat pocket, Mohammad raised the weapon and pointed it at Schmidt. Schmidt threw his hands up in front of him and screamed for the man to wait, that this was all a mistake.

The pistol roared. The bullet struck the East German through the right hand, shattering his wrist. The second hit him just above the elbow and sent Schmidt spinning into the wall and then to the floor. Moaning in extreme pain, tears filling his eyes, Schmidt pleaded with the Arab, who now stood over him, pointing the gun to his head. Schmidt closed his eyes and waited for the fatal round to be fired.

A burst of machine-gun fire erupted in the small confines of the room. Schmidt opened his eyes in time to see the Arab's pistol fall from his hand as he grabbed at his chest. Blood smeared the front of his shirt and flowed from his mouth as he pitched sideways before crumpling to the floor next to the terrified German.

"Oh, my God! My God!" cried Schmidt as he tried to crawl away from the dead man. Someone was shouting orders in both German and Russian. Schmidt looked up and saw two men in dull gray suits standing at the end of his desk, staring down at him.

"Get the bastard to his feet," said the taller of the two men.

Two East German soldiers assisted the wounded man to his feet and dumped him roughly in a chair. Schmidt screamed in pain as his shattered hand and arm banged against the corner of the desk and the arm of the chair. He almost passed out. He felt that he was about to vomit. The pain was unbelievable. Looking up, he tried to focus his eyes before asking, "Who are you peo—"

The tall man's hand shot out like a whip and slapped him across the face. "Shut up, you son of a bitch! You will not speak until I say so. I am Ivan Broski of the KGB. You are under arrest for treason, drug dealing, and assisting in terrorism against the people's state."

The pain Schmidt had experienced was quickly replaced by panic and fear at hearing the words KGB, the Russian equivalent of the CIA. Drug dealing? Terrorism? What in the world was this man saying? Schmidt looked at the man in disbelief as he said, "I don't know what you are talking about."

The denial only served to bring another slap from the KGB man. "You lie, Herr Schmidt! We have proof that you have been selling illegal chemicals to various terrorist groups in the Middle East. You had a shipment depart Denmark only yesterday. That ship is being stopped and searched by our navy at this very moment. They have instructions to remove the cargo and return it to East Germany. If they discover what we suspect, there shall be no question as to your involvement in the drug business. The charges of terrorism are undeniable as evidenced by the dead men in this office. You are a traitor to your country and the Party as well, Comrade Schmidt. Fortunately, there are those who are still loyal." The man waved to the outer office. Looking back at Schmidt with contempt in his eyes, he said, "You might have continued with your vile business if not for the loyalty of a true Russian comrade."

Broski stepped aside so that Rudolf Schmidt could see the man who had brought his dreams of wealth and early retirement to an end. Tears filled the East German's eyes to overflowing. A low moan escaped his trembling lips as he lowered his head on his chest. Standing in the doorway was Herman Schmidt—his eldest son.

CHAPTER 5

1200 hours—June 20
Abacki Pass, Afghanistan

Mikal stood in the noonday sun and watched as Abdul Khalig approached. He was alone and riding a fine black stallion this time. The two cases of money sat beside the young Russian officer. The same safety procedures he had used before were in effect at this meeting as well. It was clear from his occasional glances toward the rocks that Abdul was aware of the fact that the two men were not alone.

Halting the horse only few yards away, Khalig dismounted and walked up to the Russian. Mikal could sense that something was different about the man this time. He did not appear as jubilant as he had at the previous two meetings. His one good eye held a certain sadness and his face showed signs of sleeplessness. "I see you have brought the money, my young friend. I had hoped that the colonel would be with you this time."

"He was detained by circumstances beyond his control. I am to pay you the final amount and personally escort his son back to Moscow. If you will be so kind as to signal your men to release the last of the prisoners, we shall be done with this business."

Khalig seemed hesitant. His one good eye looked away from

Mikal and to the side of the mountain. His voice was low and sad as he said, "Your colonel loves his son very much, does he not?"

"Yes," said Mikal, expecting the rebel's next words to be a demand for more money.

"I, too, had sons at one time, three fine young boys. They are all dead now. I do wish that Colonel Molotov could have been here." Abdul paused, as a pained expression crossed his face. "The colonel has been an honorable man throughout this affair. He is not like the others I have had to deal with. He wanted nothing for himself, only for others. That is why the news I now carry causes me so much pain. You see, Lieutenant, the prize for which your commander has risked so much no longer exists."

Mikal stepped back slowly. His voice was anxious. "Wha— what are you saying? What do you mean—no longer exists? What have you done with Lieutenant Yuri Molotov?"

Khalig could still not bring himself to look the Russian in the eyes. Running the reins of the horse through his hands slowly, he stared down at the ground as he answered, "It was not I, nor my people that caused this tragic set of circumstances. It was the Afghan government troops. They attacked the camp where the prisoners were being held. We were able to save four of them—but—the colonel's son was killed when he stepped on a mine as we fled. I had my men bring the body and the four survivors with them. I know that is of little comfort, but at least he can bury him at home. I—I am sorry that this thing has happened—but the will of Allah will be done and no man can change it."

Mikal stood silent. Tears welled up in his young eyes for he knew the pain that this would bring to the very heart of his beloved commander. All their work and the risks they had taken were all to save Yuri. And now, it was all over. They had been so close. Mikal did not know what to say.

"I shall release the remaining four men. There will be no need for you to pay for them. You may keep your money. I did not live up to my part of the bargain," said Abdul as he turned and mounted his horse.

Mikal looked down at the money. It seemed so unimportant

now. He glanced up at Abdul, who had removed the mirror and signaled his men to release the prisoners. As he was replacing the glass in his robe, Mikal stepped forward, reached up, and handed the Afghan the two bags, saying, "You, sir, are also an honorable man. The deal was for the return of the Russians you held captive. You have done as we agreed. I am certain my colonel would want you to have this. I thank you for the families of those who have been returned."

Abdul Khalig paused before taking the money bags and hooking them onto his saddle. Mikal thought he saw a tear in the rebel's eye as he said, "Tell your colonel he shall be in my prayers." The Afghan spurred the horse and rode away.

Mikal's radio came alive with the verification that four Russian soldiers and the body of a fifth wrapped in silk robes had just cleared the Russian border. He acknowledged the report.

Standing alone in the heat of the rock and sand of the valley floor, Mikal dropped to his knees and wept.

1800 hours—June 20
Medina estate

The hours of waiting for word of Mikal's mission had all but frayed the nerves of Colonel Molotov. The fact that Arias had sobered up and had been severely reprimanded by Medina did little to lift the Colonel's spirits. Yanko had tried to ease the tension by reassurances that all was fine and that Yuri was probably just as worried about his father.

Standing alone on the patio overlooking the huge coffee fields that stretched as far as the eye could see, Molotov prayed that Yanko was right. Medina joined him. He carried two glasses of rum and Coke.

"Here, my friend. You look as if you could use a drink. Nothing troubles the mind quite as much as waiting."

Molotov nodded and took the drink. He asked, "Señor Medina, perhaps you can answer a question for me. Why drugs? You already have all of this. The coffee alone would provide a fortune on a yearly basis, not to mention the cattle, the horses, and the rubber plantation I saw on the way in."

"Sí, mi coronel, those things would provide for some, I suppose, but they take much work and long hours of administrating. And for what? A pittance compared to cocaine. Do you know that I can make as much off one shipment of cocaine as this entire hacienda makes in one year? No, Colonel, this is all no more than a smoke screen for my primary business, cocaine. However, I must admit, when the United States managed to engineer that international ban on certain chemicals to South America, and the Colombian government began their war on the cartel, I seriously thought we were finished. I had to spend a fortune to reestablish my processing labs across the border in Brazil and to pay all the necessary officials to ensure its safe operation. Even that would not have worked had it not been for your timely arrival, Colonel. Without those shipments of yours, the operation would have come to a standstill. Now I am in a position to become the sole leader of the drug empire, and I owe that success to you, sir. One must watch out for oneself, Colonel. *Ala salud!*" said Medina, lifting his glass in a toast.

Molotov was in no position to tell the fat man what he really thought of him and his business. Lifting his drink, he said, *"Salud."*

Yanko appeared at the double French doors that led to the patio. There was a smile on his face. "Colonel, you have a phone call, sir. It is Mikal."

Molotov stepped around Medina and moved to the phone. There was something in Yanko's voice that bothered the colonel, but he kept his face impassive as he picked up the phone.

Mikal tried to control his emotions as he spoke. Following the exchange, he was informed through one of Molotov's contacts in East Germany of the incident at the Schmidt chemical plant in Erfurt. The last shipment had been confiscated and would not be in Macapá on the twenty-second as planned.

Molotov, demonstrating his years of experience in dealing with sudden situations, continued the discussion on the phone without the slightest hint that anything was wrong.

Medina and Arias sat quietly at the bar pretending to ignore the conversation. Molotov knew they were taking in every word.

"And how is Yuri?" asked the colonel.

Mikal paused only a moment before answering. Until that second, he was not sure what he was going to say. He decided it was best that the colonel not know the truth for the time being. He would have more than enough on his mind trying to get out of the country once Medina found out there would be no third shipment.

"He is fine, Colonel. A little weak, but anxious to see you. I hope that will be soon, Colonel. I will be back in Brazil by tomorrow morning. Would you like me to bring a few friends along?" asked Mikal.

"No. That will not be necessary, Mikal. Yanko and I are being well entertained by our gracious host. There is no need for you to return. We will check the last shipment and then be on our way home. You have done well, Mikal. Thank you. Tell Yuri I will see him in a few days. Good-bye."

Hanging up the phone, Molotov joined the men at the bar.

"Good news, I take it," said Medina.

"Yes, my son has been away for a while and has just returned. He is in Moscow," said Molotov, looking at Yanko.

"So, you'll be leaving us soon, then," said Arias with a hint of glee in his voice.

"Yes, Señor Arias. I'm afraid our chance for a rematch at the bar will be out of the question. I am rather tired, now, so if you gentlemen will excuse me, I think I will retire for the evening."

"Of course, Colonel," said Medina. "Maybe tomorrow we can discuss the possibilities of future shipments through your contacts. There is much more money to be made, my friend."

Yanko was already heading up the stairs as Molotov answered, "Yes, Señor Medina, the more I have thought of our conversation on the patio, the more I have come to realize that perhaps you are right. One must watch out for oneself first. Good night, gentlemen."

Molotov told Yanko of the trouble in Erfurt as soon as they went upstairs. Mikal had specifically identified the KGB as the driving force behind the raid on Schmidt's plant, but as of yet, they had not made the connection between Molotov and the cargo. Schmidt would be tortured until he confessed to every bit of information about the people with whom he had been conducting his illegal business. Although Schmidt did not know Molotov's true identity, there was still the outside chance that the KGB would somehow link the release of the Russians along the Afghan border with the illegal cargo bound for Brazil. He would have to get back to Moscow as quickly as possible and detour any information or evidence that might point to him in the KGB investigation.

Yanko reminded him that the KGB was not their only problem. The first and most immediate danger was going to be their host. Carlos Medina had already paid for a shipment that was not going to arrive at Macapá, and both Russians had a good idea that the fat man was not going to take that very well—no, not well at all. They were going to have to get out of the country, and do so without arousing the suspicions of the drug lord.

Molotov spent the entire night plotting their escape. That morning at breakfast he informed Medina that he would have to travel to the city of Manaus to clear up a few details involving the final shipment. As an added incentive for Medina to let them go, Molotov suggested that his main contact for the East German connection was in Manaus, and that he would try to convince him that they should continue the chemical business on a monthly basis.

This excited Medina. If he could be guaranteed a monthly supply, there would be no doubt that he would be the drug king of the world. He quickly agreed with Molotov. The plane had already been prepared for the trip to Macapá. It was scheduled for the following morning. There was no sense in waiting. Arias and three of his men would go with Molotov and Yanko to the airport at Manaus. They would spend the night in the city, then they would all fly on to Macapá the following morning.

It was not what Molotov had wanted, but to object to the arrangement would have cast unwanted suspicion on the two

Russians. Arias was already voicing his distrust of Molotov. Therefore, the colonel agreed to the plan.

Medina waved them a final farewell as the twin-engine plane lifted off the dirt runway and headed for the city of Manaus, Brazil. Once in the city, Molotov planned to elude Arias and his men and arrange his own transportation out of the country.

It was 9:00 A.M. They had only to relax for now. In four hours they would be rid of Arias and be on their way home to Russia and Yuri.

0900 hours—June 21
Santo Antoñio do Içá, Brazil

Sergeant Odie Watson looked at his watch, then gazed across the small plaza at the long line of patients standing outside the makeshift medical clinic the Air Force team had set up in front of the church. They had arrived in Santo Antoñio do Içá on the seventeenth. Their stay in the small town had been scheduled for only seventy-two hours, but Captain Longly had requested and had received permission from the American Military Advisory Group at the embassy to extend their stay an additional twenty-four hours. Watson had tried, unsuccessfully, to convince the young woman that there were just too many people and not enough supplies. She could not play Sister Theresa to the entire country. It was bad enough that she had convinced General J. J. Johnson and SOCOM to lengthen the team's tour in this giant rain forest an additional month.

"At least she gave that cute little ass of hers a little more breathing room," mumbled Watson to himself as he popped down two headache pills and crossed the square to remind his attractive commander that the helicopter would be returning to pick them up at noon for their trip to Manaus. He hoped she wouldn't ask for another extension—one more day and the square would be packed to overflowing.

It wasn't that Odie Watson didn't enjoy his work. He'd been a medic for over fifteen years. No one had more compassion for the sick and injured than this man who had grown up a poor black youth from the rural area around the racist hotbed of Selma, Alabama. At the age of ten, he had stood next to his mother's bed with his five brothers and four sisters and watched helplessly as the woman, who had literally worked herself to death, died of pneumonia for the simple want of a doctor. There were no black physicians in the area then, and white doctors refused to administer to niggers. Those few who tried to uphold the Hippocratic oath and look beyond color were soon visited by the white-sheeted Ku Klux Klan, who forced them to leave not only the town, but also the state.

His mother's death had instilled in Watson a desire and a determination to enter a field where he could eventually serve not only his black brothers and sisters, but all people, everywhere. It was what his mother would have wanted. The Air Force had given him that chance. He had served two years in Vietnam flying chase medic for downed pilots and shot-up recon teams. He had worked in the hot and humid medical tents of Honduras, the mission hospitals of El Salvador, and had been with the invasion troops on the night the U.S. went in after Manuel Noriega.

No, there was no more compassionate man in the Air Force, none who more fully understood the suffering of people than Watson. He was the perfect choice to accompany a new medical officer on her first Civic Action medical mission. As of yet, he had failed to get her to understand that as long as these people of the forest and mountains knew they were here, they would continue to come, some from as far away as a hundred miles. Having to make that trek through the jungles and the mountains of Brazil was no easy task. Many of those who began the trip would not live to complete it, dying along the way.

Therein lay the problem: For all of her caring and concern for these people, by her continued presence here, she was unintentionally causing the death of many of those she had come to help. No one was more aware of that than Watson. They would have to leave at noon today. Once the chopper lifted the team out of the area, word of their departure would spread up and down the trails and rivers to the hundreds that were already on their way. They would return to their homes and await word of the arrival of another team, whenever and wherever that might be.

Sergeant Tom Foley, a tall, thin, redheaded kid from Maine, looked up as Watson approached. "Hey, Top! Boy, we're really packing them in today."

Watson looked back at the line that had increased by twenty people in the time it had taken him to cross the square. "Yeah. Well, at eleven o'clock we start packin' up our shit. Chopper'll be in here at noon. Don't you be draggin' your feet when they get in, or I'll leave your long lanky ass here. You got it?"

Foley grinned, showing a pearly white-toothed teenage smile as he nodded. Laughing, he replied, "Sure enough, Top, but I don't think you'd leave anybody here. You're too softhearted."

"Shee-it! Don't ya be bettin' your young skinny ass on it, boy. I might have some relatives livin' out there in them jungles who'd love to put that red head of yours on a stick," said Watson with a smile as he walked past Foley.

Locating Captain Longly, he joined her at her table. She smiled.

"Morning, Sergeant Watson. My Lord, did you see that line out there? Where in the world are they all coming from?"

Watson busied himself filling syringes with smallpox vaccine as he replied, "The mountains and every little village along the banks of the Amazon River, Captain. They know the Americans are here, and they'll keep coming because we stayed longer than we were supposed to. They figure if enough of 'em show up, we'll stay even longer."

Longly paused before giving an Indian woman her shot. Looking over at the senior sergeant, she noted the irritation in Watson's tone. "You're saying this crowd is my fault, Sergeant Watson?"

He didn't bother to look up. "Yes, ma'am, sure is. Told you yesterday I didn't think it was a good idea. We ain't got near enough supplies to handle this many folks, and you can bet there's more on the way."

Captain Longly looked out over the plaza. Sergeant Watson was right. More-and more people were filtering out of the jungles and into the square, some walking, others being carried on stooped backs or on litters. So many people in need of help and all here because of her. "What have I done?" she asked with a hint of remorse.

"Oh, Captain, it ain't your fault, really. Ya just got a big heart, and ya care too much. Ain't nothing wrong with that. We'll just do the best we can till the supplies run out, then head back to Manaus when the chopper comes in."

"What about them?" she asked, nodding toward the new arrivals coming out of the jungle.

"Oh, they'll be disappointed—sure. But these folks are used to disappointment. It's nothing new for them. We been running this CA program for five years now. They know we'll be back—and so will they."

Longly turned away and gave the woman her shot as Sergeants Cochran and Foster came to the insulated boxes next to the table and removed the last four boxes of vaccine from the hot-ice containers. It was just as well, thought Watson. No sense in prolonging it. Once those were gone, that was it.

"Sergeant Watson."

Watson placed the last syringe from his box on the stainless steel tray and turned to look into Longly's emerald eyes. He could tell she was about to cry. "Yes, ma'am?"

"This was another reason you didn't want me to extend our tour, isn't it?"

Watson could see the hurt in her eyes. She was young, and this was her first mission. She wanted so badly to help them all, but that was impossible. The realization was proving to be very painful.

"Yes, ma'am, it is. You see, Captain, in a war there's that pain that goes all over ya when you try your damnedest to save a kid that's been hit, but he don't make it. Well, it ain't much different out here. It's just another kind of war, that's all. Us against years of disease and sickness, and when we do all we can and we have to look into the faces of those we can't help, we feel kinda like we lost them, too. The pain's the same. It can get to you real quick, if you let it."

He watched as a small tear made its way down her smooth cheek. Placing her hand over his, she whispered, "Thank you, Odie."

The crusty old veteran patted her hand gently as he answered, "You're doin' fine, Captain. Don't you worry none."

Wiping the tear from her cheek, she went back to work. Watson opened a new box of needles, pausing only long enough to wipe away the water that had built up in his own eyes. Now, he was no different than Cochran, Foster, or Foley. The little captain had captured his heart.

1245 hours—June 21
Manaus Airport, Brazil

Molotov and Yanko stretched cramped muscles as they stepped from the small plane onto the tarmac of the Manaus Airport. Yanko motioned toward the chain link fence that surrounded the airstrip. Paramilitary and local federal police, carrying automatic rifles, patrolled the perimeter. Although Brazil was often thought of as a democracy, there was definitely a military political structure, which was not surprising when one considered that nearly every leader of Brazil for the last fifty years had been an active duty or retired general.

Molotov noted the weapons being carried by the guards, American M-16s. The United States and Brazil had enjoyed a friendly relationship for years, until the Carter presidency. President Carter's Human Rights policies and denunciation of the country's militarism had seriously damaged that relationship. Reagan had tried to reestablish the earlier ties through increased financial aid, which Brazil accepted, but the closeness that had been there before no longer existed.

Arias was talking with the pilot when a paramilitary officer came through the gates. Molotov noticed the patch on the man's right shoulder. It was the insignia of the Amazon Military Command for the eighth military region, whose headquarters were in Manaus. It was one of the units he had heard Medina bragging about having on his payroll. Two of the local police approached with the officer. They walked over to Arias. Molotov had a sudden premonition that something was wrong. He couldn't explain it. It was a sixth sense born of years of experience.

The officer stood speaking in muffled Spanish to Arias. Molotov managed to pick up parts of the conversation. There was an urgent phone call for Arias from Colombia. Instinctively, Arias looked over at Molotov and Yanko.

"Who is it?" Arias asked.

The officer did not know, but he had been informed to detain all the personnel who had arrived on the plane until Arias had had a chance to talk with the caller. This news brought a wicked smile to the Colombian's face as he again stared at Molotov. Ordering his men to keep an eye on the two Russians, Arias left for the terminal with the officer.

As they went through the gates, the two local policemen removed their rifles from their shoulders and took up positions on either side of the gate. They were to allow no one in or out. Arias's men began to spread out around Molotov and Yanko, keeping their hands near their coats and their eyes locked on the two men.

Across the runway, a helicopter was about to land. Molotov pointed in that direction as Yanko turned, shading his eyes against the noonday sun. The colonel whispered, "Something is wrong. There is little doubt that the call is from Medina. Somehow he has found out about the shipment. If we do not make our move now, we may never get another chance. Are you ready, Yanko?"

Yanko pointed to the five people who had just emerged from the chopper. They were dressed in battle fatigues. One of them was a black man. "Yes, Colonel. I shall take the man on the right and the two at the gate."

Molotov agreed. The two Russians stood with their backs to the proposed targets. Their gun hands still shaded their eyes as if they were watching the people disembark from the helicopter. Their hands dropped, and at exactly the same time they turned, one right, one left. In those few seconds, they pulled their weapons and faced the startled bodyguards, who now grabbed for their guns. They were too late. Molotov fired one shot from his Czech CZ-75 9mm pistol, which exploded the face of the man nearest him. Yanko dropped to one knee and pumped two slugs into a man near the wing. Then he shifted his aim to the two federal policemen at the gate, unleashing five rapid shots before they could react. One pitched forward with two holes in his chest. The other man was knocked backward by the impact of the other three bullets that tore through his abdomen, throat, and chest.

Molotov's second target managed to level his Mac-10 machine pistol and fire a short burst that was low and to the right of the colonel. Molotov never flinched as the stream of bullets sparked their way past him. Calmly, he took aim and shot the man between the eyes. In a matter of seconds, it was over. Five men lay dead on the tarmac.

"Yanko! Come—across the runway!" yelled Molotov as he saw more police and soldiers running toward the gates.

The two Russians broke into a dead run across the field, neither one taking the time to look back. They knew what was there. Molotov watched the people who had arrived on the chopper go into a small hangar just beyond the helicopter pad. It was a way to escape. A siren began to blare. Series of shots rang out from behind them. Bullets ricocheted off the concrete on either side of the fleeing men.

Yanko was in the lead and nearing the hangar when two policemen suddenly appeared in the doorway of the building. Not sure of what was happening, the two still had their weapons slung on their shoulders. Yanko didn't even slow down. The Beretta bucked four times, and the two men went down. Darting through the hangar, the two exited onto the street and stopped to catch their breaths. From the main terminal, Molotov saw the flashing blue lights of the military jeeps racing toward them. To his right a hotel van was just pulling away from the curb.

"Yanko! The van. Hurry!"

Both men ran up alongside the van. Yanko jerked the side doors open and both men leaped inside. Molotov thought he heard a startled woman's voice as he slammed into one of the metal ends of a seat. The driver stomped on the brake and sent the colonel spilling forward on his back between the seats. The wide-eyed driver looked down at Molotov and saw the gun in the old man's hands.

"Drive!" yelled Yanko.

The Brazilian was shaking in terror. Opening his door, he jumped out of the van and ran away.

"Goddamn it! What's going on here?" yelled Watson as he rose from his seat.

Yanko extended his arm with the barrel of his gun no less than a foot from Watson's face. "Shut up and sit down!" said Yanko. The sergeant obeyed. Shifting the gun to Airman Foley, Yanko screamed, "You! Get up there and drive. Now!"

The redhead was mesmerized by the size of the hole at the end of the barrel leveled at him. He had never realized how big a gun barrel really was until now.

Yanko thumbed back the hammer on the automatic as he screamed, "Do it, damn you! Or I'll blow your brains out right here."

Foley scrambled past the man and climbed behind the wheel. Swinging the van out into the traffic, he asked, "Where am I supposed to drive to?"

"Just drive!" said Yanko, his words coming in short gasps.

Molotov, his back now resting against a seat, was still trying to catch his breath from his quarter-mile race across the field. Sweat was stinging his eyes. There was a slight pain in his chest and left arm. Yanko knelt down beside him with concern. He asked, "Are you hit, Colonel?"

Molotov couldn't speak. He shook his head no. There was a sudden movement of one of the passengers. Yanko swung the Beretta to the rear of the van. The sight came to rest on an attractive young woman. She was pulling a small oxygen bottle from a gray Air Force kit bag that lay at her feet.

"What are you doing?" asked Yanko.

"He needs oxygen," she said as she moved forward, knelt, and placed the mask over the colonel's face. After she activated the valve, Molotov immediately began to breathe more easily. For the first time, Yanko noticed the twin silver bars on the woman's collar.

"Who are you people?" asked Longly.

"That does not matter, Captain," replied Yanko. "We will not detain you long. We need only to get as far away from this area as possible." Pausing, Yanko looked at her, then at the three men in the rear of the van. "You are Americans, yes?" It was more of a statement than a question.

"Ya bet your sweet ass we are!" said Watson. "United States

Air Force. You fuck with us, and you're fuckin' with Uncle Sam. You oughta think about that, sonny. Now, I don't know who you two guys are, but you sure as hell ain't terrorists. Unless that ol' guy is a refugee from an old terrorist rest home. He's old enough to be my ol' man. So what's the game, and how come we're playin'?"

Yanko recognized the rank on Watson's collar. "It is no game, Sergeant. As I have said, we need only to get away from this area. Once we have accomplished that, you will be free to go."

Molotov pushed the mask away. "Thank you, Captain. I am fine now. Please return to your seat."

Leaving the bottle where it was, Longly returned to her place beside Watson.

Molotov pulled himself up into the passenger seat across from Foley while Yanko sat directly behind the driver with his gun covering the others. The traffic was beginning to thin out as the van approached the edge of town. Looking out the back window, Molotov could no longer see the flashing blue lights of the military police jeeps. They just might make it after all.

As Foley rounded a curve, he shouted, "Holy shit!"

The main road was blocked with no fewer than ten jeeps. Soldiers were everywhere. Molotov cursed under his breath. There was a dirt road going off to the right. "Turn here!" he said.

Foley obeyed and turned onto the side road. He had only driven a hundred yards when he yelled, "No good! There are people on the road. They're—"

A hail of bullets shattered the windshield as Molotov and the others dove for the floor. Foley screamed once as a bullet ripped through his right shoulder and another found its way along his right side. His scream was quickly silenced by a third and fatal bullet that struck the young airman above the left eye, exploding his head, sending blood and brains along the roof of the van.

The vehicle swerved out of control and slammed into a ditch beside the road. Yanko kicked open the doors and jumped out. Bullets smashed the door windows showering slivers of glass into his face.

Patrica Longly pulled herself up from the floor to see the horribly disfigured head of Airman Foley. The bloody mess on the ceiling of the van made her clutch at her stomach, trying desperately not to vomit. She lost the battle.

Two soldiers rushed toward the van. Yanko dove for the ditch, firing as he rolled. Both men fell dead in the road.

Molotov, stunned, staggered from the van. He was shot immediately in the right arm, just above the elbow. He spun sideways into the side of the van and fell to the dirt.

"Colonel!" yelled Yanko as he tried to wipe the streams of blood flowing into his eyes. Another soldier peeked around the van and raised his rifle. Yanko blew his head apart as he dashed over to grab the colonel. His hands just gripped the colonel's shirt when two rounds struck Yanko in the chest, driving him back against the van. His shirtsleeve hung on the sideview mirror preventing him from falling to the ground.

Patrica Longly, having just thrown up, felt another wave coming on as she stared in disbelief at the young Russian officer who was being shot to pieces before her eyes. Round after round jerked and tore at Yanko's body. Watson put his hand over the young woman's eyes and lowered her head in the seat. She didn't need to see that. She had already seen too much.

Molotov fought back the searing pain that gripped his shattered arm as he tried to crawl over to his weapon. His hand touched the grips just as a shoe stomped down hard on his fingers. Uttering a low moan, he looked up through pain-crazed eyes to see Arias staring down at him with a wide, toothy grin.

"I knew you were a bastard the first day I met you, Colonel. Now, we shall see if you are as hard a man as you would have people believe. Carlos Medina does not take kindly to those who steal from him, and that was what you had in mind, wasn't it, you Russian pig. You think you military idiots are the only ones with an intelligence network? You knew the final shipment had been confiscated, didn't you?" Arias pressed his shoe down harder on the colonel's fingers. "I shall enjoy watching Medina kill you slowly, you old bastard."

Arias lifted his foot and stepped back as he jacked a round

into the chamber of the .380 pistol he held in his hand. "But before he has his fun with you, I deserve a little of my own for the trouble you have caused me." Pointing the weapon at Molotov's head, the Colombian laughed, then he swung the pistol down to the old man's legs and fired at point-blank range. Molotov screamed as the bullet shattered his right kneecap.

"Stop it! Stop it, damn you!" screamed Captain Longly as she jumped from the van, attempting to grab Arias by the arm. The Colombian delivered a vicious backhand across the woman's mouth, knocking her to the ground.

"Motherfucker!" yelled Watson as he pulled away from the two soldiers holding him by the arms. Swinging his left fist, he caught Arias square on the jaw with enough force to break one of the man's teeth. Arias fell hard to the ground. One of the soldiers quickly raised the butt of his rifle and hit Watson in the back of the head, knocking him unconscious. Cochran and Foster made a move to help their fallen comrade, but they quickly received a series of butt strokes and kicks from the soldiers around them that drove them to the ground.

Helping Arias to his feet, an officer asked, "What do we do with the Americanos?"

Wiping the blood from his lip and grimacing from the pain of the broken tooth, Arias stepped over and kicked Watson in the side of the head before saying, "Take them all to the airfield. For all we know, they could have been in on this with that damn Russian. Medina will know what to do with them."

"What of the driver and this one?" asked the officer, pointing to the mutilated body of Yanko, still dangling from the side mirror.

Looking back over his shoulder as he walked away, Arias replied, "Feed them to the piranha."

CHAPTER 6

2330 hours—June 21
MacDill AFB, Tampa Bay

The phone rang for a fourth time before B. J. Mattson realized he wasn't dreaming. Still half asleep, he reached across the bed and fumbled for the receiver.

"Hel—hello."

"B.J.—General Johnson. We've got a hot one going down. Get yourself together and be in my office in ten minutes."

At the sound of the general's voice, B.J.'s eyes shot open. He was instantly awake. "Yes, sir. On my way. Out."

Swinging himself out of bed, he headed straight for the shower. Three minutes under the icy water vanquished the sound sleep of only minutes ago. Pulling a set of fatigues from the closet, B.J. threw them on with the precision of a man accustomed to dressing in a hurry. Lacing up his boots, he thought of the sense of urgency he had noted in Q-Tip's voice. The old man wasn't one to overreact to anything. Whatever was going down tonight had J. J. Johnson worried.

Tying the bootlaces, Mattson grabbed his green beret off the dresser and ran out the door. He hoped the general hadn't been serious about his being there in ten minutes—it was going to take him fifteen.

2345 hours—June 21
General Sweet's residence
MacDill AFB

"Raymond! Raymond, wake up. It's the phone," said Doris Sweet as she continued tapping her snoring husband on the shoulder.

"Wha—what? Oh, yes. Okay, I'll get it."

Switching on the lamp on the nightstand, Sweet rubbed his eyes. Picking up the phone, he said, "General Sweet here."

Sweet immediately recognized the gruff voice on the other end of the line. It was Major General John Garland, Sweet's boss, and the primary reason Sweet had been selected as Johnson's deputy. The two men were both conventional officers and had graduated from West Point together. Garland's dislike for Special Operations units was well known in Washington and the Pentagon.

"Raymond, this is John Garland. What's going on down there?"

Sweet wasn't sure if he was still asleep or if he just didn't understand the question. "What? What do you mean? Going on where, John?"

Garland was irritated. "Goddamn it, man. You mean to tell me you have no idea what I'm talking about?"

"Well, uh—no. I can't say I do, John."

"Raymond, correct me if I'm wrong, but it is my understanding that you were placed in that plush-ass job down there in a sunny paradise to keep an eye on J. J. Johnson and his gang of Rambo delinquents, isn't that right?"

Sweet was still trying to figure out what the man was talking about. "Well, yes, that's right, John, and I'm doing just that." Sweet paused. There was no reply. He wondered if his boss was feeling all right. It sounded as if Garland were hyperventilating.

"Uh, John, I said, that's right. You still there, John? By the way, I've been meaning to talk to you about Major Mattson. I have a suspicion the man has been doctoring orders that—"

Garland's voice boomed so loud that Sweet had to hold the phone away from his ear. "Shut up, Raymond! Listen! You get your ass out of that bed and over to SOCOM Headquarters. Something is going on, but I don't know what it is yet. No one here is talking, but I have reliable information that the secretary of defense was at the White House to see the president less than an hour ago with three members of the Senate Intelligence Committee. The Air Force boys at Andrews received a call from the president himself to have a plane readied for a flight to Tampa. They'll be carrying four passengers. One will be the secretary. Raymond, you get your butt over there. I want to know who gets off that plane, what they're doing there, and how Johnson and his G.I. Joe heroes are involved. You understand, Raymond?"

Sweet was fully awake now. "Yes, sir, I understand. Who, what, where, and why. Got it, John."

Garland's voice took on a sadistic tone that gave Sweet a chill down his back. "Raymond, you fuck this up and I promise you, I'll have your ass living in an igloo in the middle of Antarctica counting goddamn penguins! Call me as soon as you have the information. Good-bye."

Sweet reached over to hang up the phone. His wife stirred in the bed and asked, "Goodness, dear, who was that?"

"John Garland," said Sweet, yawning.

Fluffing her pillow, Doris Sweet's words faded as she said, "I know you two are the best of friends, Raymond, but really, you should talk to the man about calling people in the middle of the night. I'm sure he'd understand—"

Sweet stood looking down at his wife. He tried to envision her wrapped in polar bear skins instead of satin sheets as he sighed saying, "Yes, of course. I'm sure he would, dear."

2400 hours—June 21
MacDill AFB

J. J. Johnson looked up from the file he was reading. Seeing B.J. in the outer office, he waved the major in. "Sit down, B.J."

Mattson noted the seriousness in the general's face as he took a seat in the oversized chair directly in front of the desk. "What have we got, General?"

"I wish the hell I knew," said Johnson. "I received a call

from the ComCenter a little past eleven. They said I had a call from Clinton Bowers. They patched him through on the secure voice phone at my house. Clinton didn't really tell me much, just that it involved our Civic Action team down in Brazil and that certain sources confirmed that one member of the team had been killed and the others abducted."

Mattson sat forward in the chair. "My God, that's Captain Longly's team."

"Exactly. However, there's more to this than Clinton cared to discuss over the phone. He is on his way here now with three other people."

"Any idea who?" asked B.J.

"He didn't say, but it must be somebody important. He wants a total security blackout around one of our hangars. None of the people on the plane will exit until the aircraft is in the hangar. Bowers doesn't want anyone else within a hundred yards of the blackout area. You and I will be the only people in that hangar when they open the doors. I've already notified Air Force security and the Air Commando team to block off hangar 3 on the north end of the strip. They're using a Lear jet out of Andrews. They should be here in about two hours."

"What about General Sweet? He's not going to take kindly to being left out of this," said Mattson.

Johnson smiled. "That's the one thing Bowers did tell me. He doesn't want Sweet within a mile of that runway. That's the secretary of defense's orders, not mine."

Major Erin Tibetts appeared in the doorway. "Got here as quickly as I could, sir."

Johnson waved him in. "That's fine, Erin. I'm going to need some computer readouts from your G-2 section. I want to know who we have in the command who has had anything to do with the Amazon Basin region of Brazil. Check them all out, SEALs, Rangers, SF, and the Air Commandos, anybody who has spent any time at all in the region. I need that list no later than two hours from now. Can you handle it, Erin?"

Tibetts grinned and said, "No problem, thanks to new age technology, sir. You got it. Anything else, sir?"

Johnson sat back in his chair, slowly rolling an unlit cigar between his lips, running the question through his mind.

Lowering the cigar, he said, "Yes, Erin, while you're at it, run me up a sheet on known insurgent groups and any terrorists that have been active lately in that area."

"Have it all in two hours, sir," said Tibetts. He saluted smartly, pivoted on his heel, and left the office.

Staring at the wet end of his cigar, the general asked, "B.J., when is Jake due back from California?"

"This weekend, sir. If you want, I can get in touch with him now and have him on the first thing smoking back this way."

"No, that's all right. Let's wait until we find out what we're up against. Having Jake in Coronado and Smitty near Fort Benning may prove to be a blessing in disguise." Johnson stood up and stretched. "What do you say to some coffee, then a trip out to the hangar to check on our security boys?"

"Sounds good," said B.J. as he stood to follow the general to the door. Glancing up at the clock on the wall of the outer office, Mattson noticed it was just past midnight. Somewhere at this very minute a Lear jet was making its way through the night sky above the east coast. In less than two hours it would dump a shit-load of trouble on SOCOM's doorstep. But then, that was their business, to handle the shit no one else could or would. After all, they were good at it.

Closing the door behind him, B.J. grinned to himself as he thought of the song that had been playing on his radio when he arrived in the parking lot. It suddenly seemed quite appropriate. Hurrying down the hall to catch up with the general, the words resounded in his mind: "After midnight, we're gonna let it all hang out."

0205 hours—June 22
Hangar 3
MacDill AFB

Q-Tip Johnson and B.J. were alone in the hangar as the side door of the executive jet opened and a ladder unfolded to the concrete. Clinton Bowers, the secretary of defense, was the first man out. Seeing his old college roommate standing off to the side, the man in his late fifties with the salt and pepper hair waved to the general as he came down the steps. The second man who stepped out behind Bowers had all the markings of a CIA type: mid-thirties, well built, suspicious of everything; he moved his head from side to side, taking in every inch of the hangar with a single glance. He wore the standard dark polyester suit and, of course, no agent was complete without his sunglasses. This man even wore them at night.

B.J. glanced over at Johnson as the man came down the stairs. The general raised an eyebrow in acknowledgment. He, too, had made the guy as an agent.

The exit of the last two men definitely attracted the two SOCOM officers' full attention. J. J. Johnson was not a man accustomed to being shocked by any set of circumstances, but he was totally unprepared for this. B.J. was equally surprised. He had just seen the shorter of the two men on television a few days ago in a CNN news report on the Russian premier's scheduled visit to the United States next month. The man's name was Boris Yelintikov, the second most powerful man in Russia. He was every bit as impressive in person as he had appeared on television. Although short, he had a stocky build and broad shoulders. His thinning hair was accented by thick, bushy eyebrows and a strong, serious face.

Neither Mattson nor Johnson recognized the last man, obviously a Russian as well. He stood six foot four and his wide shoulders tapered down to a narrow waist. His dull gray suit had been poorly altered to accommodate his massive biceps and powerful legs. Whoever this guy was, he sure as hell wasn't a desk jockey in some executive office of the Kremlin. His every calculated move and the way he carried himself left little doubt that this was a man of few words and plenty of action. As the party gathered around B.J. and the general, Bowers began the introductions.

"General Johnson, Major Mattson, may I present our visitors." Singling out the man with sunglasses first, he said, "This is Mr. Brian Ballock. Mr. Ballock is with the Central Intelligence Agency." Ballock's glasses remained in place as he shook hands with the two officers. B.J. thought about asking the man for an autograph, but let the idea go.

Turning to the Russians, Bowers began with the shorter man first. "Gentlemen, this is Mr. Boris Yelintikov, Mr. Gorbachev's right-hand man and soon to be next president of the Russian republic."

Yelintikov flashed a disarming smile and shook hands with the two officers. In flawless English he said, "It is a pleasure to meet you, gentlemen."

"Likewise, I assure you, sir," replied Johnson.

Bowers introduced the next man. "And this is Lieutenant Colonel Alexei Karpov."

Johnson nodded as he shook the big man's hand.

B.J. reached out to take the oversized hand in his own just as Bowers added, "Colonel Karpov is the senior instructor of the Spetsnaz Special Forces School at Furstenburg, East Germany."

Out of instinct, B.J. quickly released the man's hand. His action was noticed by those around them. The Spetsnaz were the Russian counterparts to the American Green Berets and Rangers. In effect, Karpov was the man who taught the Soviet Special Forces troops how to track down and kill the Special Operations people under General J. J. Johnson's command. Mattson's eyes shifted to Bowers with a questioning look. Just what in the hell was this man doing here?

Karpov's English was as good as that of Mr. Yelintikov.

"Your name is not unfamiliar to me, Major Mattson," said the tall Russian. His dark brown eyes watched for B.J.'s reaction as he spoke. "I have seen it mentioned a number of times in our reports. I believe you often work with a Navy commander, a Lieutenant Commander Mortimer. Is that correct?"

B.J. stared back at the man. Though only standing a few feet apart, the tension between these two warriors could be felt by those around them.

"I'm flattered, Colonel. It's always nice to hear that one's work is appreciated," B.J. replied.

Clinton Bowers cleared his throat and said, "Uh—Jonathan, I have to apologize for the rather abrupt way this was handled. Normally I would have had you and Major Mattson come to the White House, but we didn't want the press in on this. There just wasn't time for formal protocol. We have a very delicate situation on our hands, and I don't mind telling you that both the president and Mr. Gorbachev are concerned."

General Johnson was still looking at the Spetsnaz colonel as he said, "You don't have to tell me that, Clinton. If it's important enough for you to bring these gentlemen to a classified installation, then it must be vital. My major concern is Captain Longly and her team."

Boris Yelintikov noticed the stainless steel coffee container sitting on a small table against one wall of the hangar. "Excuse me, please, Mr. Secretary, but would it be possible for us to have some coffee before we begin our explanations of this affair?"

"Of course, sir," replied Bowers. Johnson started to object. Having some of his people in trouble might not bother the Russian, but it sure as hell bothered him. Bowers saw the objection on his friend's face. "General Johnson, coffee sounds like a very good idea." The general knew he had just been told to cool it for now.

With their coffee cups filled, the group sat around a large table while Bowers began again. "Jonathan, I'm afraid we have a situation that could have widespread international ramifications, should it become public knowledge. Unfortunately, it has already cost the lives of two men. One, a Russian officer of the Spetsnaz, and the other, an American airman with your Air Force Civic Action team in Brazil."

Q-Tip lowered his head and stared at the tabletop as he asked, "It wasn't Captain Longly was it, Clinton?"

"No, Jonathan. It was one of the men."

"Terrorists or—" Johnson paused purposely to stare across at Karpov as he asked, "Communist guerrillas?"

Yelintikov seemed flustered by the remark, while Karpov's expression never changed.

"Neither, General," said Bowers quickly. "They were innocent victims caught up in a running gun battle between two Russian officers and a drug lord's gunmen."

Mattson's head shot up. His eyes riveted on Yelintikov.

"Drugs! Well, so much for fucking glasnost and detente. I thought Mr. Gorbachev made a big deal out of that subject before the United Nations a few months ago, preaching about a united world putting an end to the drug trade and all that crap. Hell, he even made minor history by having his ambassador to the UN vote with the United States for a change on the international ban on illegal chemicals to the drug-producing countries. Now we find out the Russians are dealing in the shit. Somehow, I'm not surprised." Mattson's concern for Captain Longly added a bitter edge to his remarks.

"Major!" said Bowers. "That will be quite enough of that. Please keep your personal opinions to yourself."

Johnson let his eyes wander down to the end of the table. Brian Ballock sat silently sipping his coffee, apparently satisfied to be only an observer. Johnson came to B.J.'s defense. "Clinton, the major's only concern is the safety of Captain Longly. Could you possibly enlighten us as to how our people became involved in this situation, and how that relates to the presence of these gentlemen?"

"Jonathan, are you familiar with the name Nikolai Molotov?" asked Bowers.

"Of course. He is to the Russians what Dorby or Bank were to our military. He is a brilliant tactician and near folk hero to the Soviet people. Are you telling me he is involved in this?"

Yelintikov raised his hand. "If I may, Mr. Secretary?"

Bowers nodded his approval.

"General Johnson, it is an honor to hear a man of your stature speak so highly of one of our countrymen. To answer your question, yes, Colonel Molotov is deeply involved in this unfortunate affair; however, not for any of the reasons one might think." Yelintikov went on to explain the circumstances surrounding Molotov's son and the recent release of the Soviet POWs by Afghan rebels. B.J. and Johnson sat intently listening to the story of how Molotov's covert operation had covered Brazil, East Germany, and Afghanistan.

He then traced the events leading up to the arrest of Herr Schmidt and the confiscation of the materials from the freighter on the high seas. It was only during the intense questioning of Schmidt that the KGB and the Soviet Intelligence branch of GRU began to piece together the Russian involvement in the drug business.

Yelintikov emphasized that it would have only been a matter

of time before the combined forces of the KGB and the GRU would have linked Colonel Molotov to the release of the POWs and the illegal chemicals being shipped to South America. Here he paused, and with an honest sadness in his voice, he said, "It would have been better for him had we found out sooner about his involvement and brought him back to Russia. At least then he could have possibly presented his case before the central committee. Many members of the committee had sons who fought in Afghanistan. I am certain they would have understood his reasons for doing what he did. Now, we fear there is little hope that he will survive this ordeal."

Both Johnson and B.J. noticed the oppressed spirit that came over Alexei Karpov as Yelintikov related the events that had brought them here. They had no way of knowing that it had been Molotov who had trained this leader of the elite Spetsnaz. He had been both his mentor and his friend.

"Why do you say that?" asked B.J. "I would think your country would be more than willing to trade anything for a national hero."

"It's not quite that simple, Major," said Bowers. You said it yourself. Gorbachev can not deliver a speech in front of the world, then turn around and provide materials for the mass production of cocaine. Put that together with his public support of the president's rule of not dealing with people who take hostages, and you have a large credibility problem in the world press."

Johnson turned to Bowers and asked, "Clinton, just what was it that Molotov was selling to this guy Medina, anyway?"

"Ether, General!" said Ballock, speaking for the first time since the introductions. "Are you familiar with the cocaine process, General?"

"Not as much as I should be," replied Johnson.

Ballock stood up and removed his sunglasses. The reasons for the glasses became quickly apparent to those at the table. There were two half-inch scars under each of his eyes. Judging from their jagged appearance, they had been made by something other than a sharp-edged object. Ballock could see the questioning looks from the two SOCOM officers. His hand instinctively went up to gently touch the twin scars. "As you

can see, General, I have firsthand knowledge of the ruthless-
ness of drug dealers. These are souvenirs from Mr. Carlos
Medina. It was my misfortune to be his guest for a few days
three years ago. They hung me upside down and used broken
glass to cut slits under my eyes. Then they filled the holes with
rock salt. They took great pleasure in raising and lowering my
head into a vat of kerosene so that I might have a greater
appreciation for the cocaine making process."

Only Karpov continued to stare at the man's scars. The
others looked away, sorry that they had made Ballock feel that
he must explain his appearance.

"Anyway, that's another story. You see, General, the
cocaine process begins with the leaves which are gathered by
the campesinos and transported to paste labs located near the
fields. There they are treated with an alkaline solution—lime
or potash—which breaks down the leaves' alkaloids, one of
which is cocaine. They are then soaked in an oil drum or
plastic vat filled with kerosene. When the alkaloids have fully
dissolved into the kerosene, the dead leaves are skimmed off
and sulfuric acid is added to the mixture. The acid interacts
with the alkaloids and forms a collection of salts, one of which
is cocaine. The kerosene is removed and more alkaline is
added to neutralize the acid. What you have left is a gummy
grayish paste. This is the coca paste. It takes a thousand
pounds of leaves to make just ten pounds of paste. The paste
gets another kerosene bath and the alkaloids sink to the bottom
of the drum. The mushy crystals left at the top are crude
cocaine, about sixty percent pure. These are washed in
alcohol, filtered, dried, then dissolved in sulfuric acid. Potas-
sium permanganate is added to destroy the non-cocaine alkaloids. Add ammomium hydroxide, filter it one more time, and
let it dry. Pure cocaine alkaloid, better known as cocaine base,
is what you have left."

"That's what addicts use when they say they've been free-
basing. Is that correct?" asked Johnson.

"Exactly, General. The base is not soluble in water. It can be
smoked or free-based, but it cannot be inhaled through the
mucous membranes of the nose. To create a powder of
crystalline salt that can be inhaled, the base must be dissolved

in ether; then it becomes a powder product. It takes seventeen liters of ether to make one kilo of cocaine," said Ballock as he returned to his seat.

"Jesus Christ," said B.J., "sulfuric acid, kerosene, and ammonium hydroxide! And people suck this stuff up their noses and shoot it in their veins."

Ballock sat back in his chair. "Ten million Americans regularly. No telling how many people worldwide. That's why there is an international ban on ether sales to Latin countries. Now, you want to hear the clincher? Before the ban, ninety percent of the ether these drug dealers used came from the U.S. and West Germany."

Yelintikov and Karpov looked critically at the Americans. Johnson was uncomfortable with the matter-of-fact statement about the U.S. Ballock, however, had left little doubt as to his expertise on the subject, after having presented such a clear picture of the cocaine process.

"So, what we have is Molotov procuring the ether from a black marketer in East Germany, having it shipped out of West Germany and Denmark, then being paid by this Colombian drug dealer named Medina. That money then was used to buy freedom for his son and other Russian soldiers being held by the Afghans. Now, is that right, or have I missed something?" asked Johnson.

Yelintikov nodded and said, "Exactly, General. Tragically, Colonel Molotov felt that our country had forsaken his son and the others. So, on his own, he organized this covert operation. Right or wrong, this man has placed our country in a very compromising position. Medina has demanded that we make good on the final shipment of ether or he will execute Colonel Molotov. He plans to film the entire affair and release the tape and the full story to the world press. Needless to say, in these times, such an incident would do little to help our image. It could have a devastating effect on the premier's efforts for world unity."

"Was he right?" asked B.J.

"About what, Major Mattson?" asked Yelintikov.

"Were you going to write his son and the others off?"

Yelintikov could feel Karpov's eyes on him. It was a

question that the Spetsnaz leader had been asking for over a year. How ironic it seemed that he would have to be sitting in a hangar in the United States to get his answer.

"Well, Major, as you know, there comes a time when one must cut his losses and move on to other things."

Johnson thought of the American POWs in Vietnam. Glancing at Bowers, he answered, "Yes, Mr. Yelintikov, we know that political point of view better than most."

Bowers looked away, not wanting to look Johnson in the eye. "So my people were caught in the middle of Molotov's escape attempt, and now this guy Medina is holding them as insurance. He hopes our president will have some influence with Mr. Gorbachev."

"That is one possibility, General. However, Colonel Karpov believes that should Medina not be able to conclude a deal with Russia, he will make good his threat to use the American prisoners to demand the same thing from your people," said Yelintikov.

That was the last thing the Americans at the table wanted to hear. The thought of turning on the television and witnessing the execution of Patrica Longly brought back bitter memories of a similar affair in the Middle East, the videotaping of an American Marine colonel hung by Arab terrorists.

"Just who in the hell is this bastard Medina, anyway?" asked B.J.

Ballock fielded the question. "Carlos Medina, age forty-five, is a native-born Colombian, the son of a peasant family. He began his career as a criminal at the age of ten. He was involved in robbery and the black market. At fifteen, he killed his first man as part of an initiation ritual to become a member of the Latin Mafia. Medina achieved full-fledged hit-man status by age twenty-one. He has been credited with thirty-two murders and suspected of twelve more. His boss was a man named Jose Petratina, a fast-rising crime lord of the early sixties. Medina became the number-one lieutenant in the organization and Petratina's right-hand man. He was responsible for handling the drug business, which at the time was just becoming a major money business. We believe it was Medina who got his boss hooked on the white powder. In 1984, he had the old man and fifteen other members of the Petratina regime murdered. He then stepped in and took the business, forcing his way into the cartel through threats and a bloody six-month gang war that was only settled when the other four drug lords in the country agreed to recognize him as the new boss of Petratina's territory. Medina is a ruthless bastard who takes sadistic pleasure in torturing his victims before killing them." Ballock paused, his fingers going up to touch the scars beneath his sunglasses.

"I can personally attest to that, gentlemen. Had it not been for the unexpected arrival of a Colombian army patrol led by American DEA agents, I would not be sitting here now."

General Johnson and B.J. looked over at each other. Their fears for Pat Longly were heightened by the CIA man's comments.

"No, gentlemen," continued Ballock, "do not underesti-mate this man. The very product that has made him a power in his own country has also brought Medina under its spell. He is a chronic user of his own white powder and it is slowly deteriorating his brain. If he says he will videotape these executions and release them to the major networks, you can be assured that he will do exactly that. Russians or Americans, men or women—it will make no difference to this man."

A long moment of silence passed over the table as Ballock finished and leaned back in his chair. The CIA man didn't talk much, but when he did, he had a way of leaving an impression on those around him. Johnson stared across at the two Russians and then at Bowers.

"Okay, Clinton, so now we know who this guy is, who he's holding, and why. However, I still fail to see why Mr. Yelintikov and Colonel Karpov are here."

Bowers stood, placed his hands in his pockets, and walked a few steps away from the table before answering. "Jonathan, you know, of course, that neither Mr. Gorbachev nor the president are going to comply with this guy's demands."

Johnson nodded and answered, "That goes without saying, Clinton."

"That only leaves our two countries with one option," said Bowers. "Colonel Karpov's group was already prepared to mount a rescue operation when an interesting and disturbing question arose. What if Colonel Molotov were rescued, but the Americans were killed in the attempt? Now, this is supposed to be a covert affair with a total press blackout. The only people who would have knowledge of such an incident and question the American deaths would be our own Congressional Intelligence Committee and, of course, our military intelligence people. I don't have to tell you, Jonathan, there are still plenty of people on the Hill who would love nothing better than to have the opportunity to point an accusing finger at the Russians and blame them for the deaths of those Americans."

Both Johnson and Mattson saw where this conversation was going.

The Secretary continued. "Likewise, should we attempt a raid and Colonel Molotov, a national hero, I might add, is accidentally killed by our team, then it would be our side that would come under criticism by the Russian politicians and certain members of their military."

B.J. interrupted. "Excuse me, Mr. Secretary, but with all due respect to my counterpart here, no one can guarantee that any of those being held will not be killed in a rescue attempt, no matter who tries it."

Colonel Karpov nodded in agreement, allowing a look of appreciation to cross his face for the respect Mattson had shown him in his statement.

"Of course, you are absolutely correct. Colonel Karpov has expressed the same opinion to our leaders in Moscow. That is why we are here," said Yelintikov.

"A joint operation," said Johnson.

"Precisely, Jonathan," replied Bowers, returning to his seat and folding his hands in front of him on the table. "They want Molotov; we want Captain Longly and the others. A joint operation demonstrates goodwill on the part of both countries and, at the same time, should misfortune befall any of the captives, neither side can blame the other."

"Let's not forget Mr. Medina, gentlemen," said Ballock. "He is already on the scoreboard. One U.S. citizen, one Russian; let's not forget that. The captives are the priority, but the destruction of Medina and his organization is equally important. The world will be a better place with the bastard six feet under. It will also send a message to the other members of the cartel."

"What do you think, Jonathan?" asked Bowers.

"The president is behind this, Clinton?"

"One hundred percent."

"What about possible leaks?" asked B.J.

"We, as well as the Russians, have taken every possible precaution, Major, although there is always that chance. But who would believe it if the story did break?" said Bowers.

"I hear that," answered Mattson. "I'm sitting right here at the table, and I'm having a hard time believing it."

Johnson looked at Yelintikov. "Sir, what kind of time limits are we looking at here?"

"Forty-eight hours, General. Our embassy in Brazil received the message at six o'clock last night. By eight o'clock, I had conferred with my superiors and contacted Mr. Bowers and your president. Fortunately, Colonel Karpov was in Cuba. Mr. Bowers made arrangements for the colonel to be flown to Washington, where we conferred with the president, and then notified you. And here we are."

"Damn," said Johnson glancing at his watch. "We've already lost nine hours. Can your people stall for more time?"

Yelintikov had anticipated the question. "Yes, General. We have already discussed that. We will wait a full thirty-six hours before replying to Medina's message. Of course, we shall agree to his conditions, but then we will request another seventy-two hours to prepare the shipment and get it on its way."

The general seemed relieved. "Okay, so we're looking at a total time span of five days, minus nine hours." Turning to B.J., he asked, "Major, how about it?"

Mattson was studying Karpov. The colonel wasn't saying anything, but it was apparent that he had already started running the timetable in his mind.

"We have done a hell of a lot more in less time, sir. It'd be tight, but I think we can handle it. Of course, I have no way of knowing the reaction time of Colonel Karpov's personnel," said B.J., looking across at the man.

A slight grin cracked at the corners of Karpov's mouth. "Six of my best men were scheduled to land in Cuba two hours ago. I have no reason to believe they are not there at this very moment."

"You were pretty sure of yourself, weren't you, Colonel?" asked Johnson.

"No, General, my men and I were going in whether a joint operation was agreed to or not. Colonel Molotov is more than just a hero to the Spetsnaz, he is our symbol—he is the Spetsnaz. My men and I are prepared to give our lives to save him. He would do no less for any of us."

The Soviet colonel didn't know it, but he had just scored some impressive points with the two SOCOM officers. Johnson excused himself and made a call from an office in the hangar. When he returned, he informed the group that he had just spoken with his G-2 at SOCOM Headquarters. They had identified ten possible candidates for the mission. The Russians were going in with a force of seven men. SOCOM would limit their selection to the same number. B. J. Mattson and Jake Mortimer would lead the team of five men selected from the list. It was now 0400 hours. SOCOM could have their people at MacDill by 1700 hours this afternoon.

In the next hour and a half, a plan was formulated. General Johnson, Boris Yelintikov, and Brian Ballock would utilize the Lear jet to fly Colonel Karpov back to Cuba. Then they would continue on to Howard Air Force Base in Panama. There they would arrange for the arrival of the Russian and American teams. Linkup in Panama was scheduled for 2100 hours tonight. After the initial briefing, the teams would be flown to a DEA/CIA-run airstrip located outside Bogotá, Colombia. Here, final intelligence would be updated and all required equipment made ready. By midnight, they would load their parachutes and depart by C-130 Blackbird. Rigging and jumpmaster checks would be conducted in flight. Infiltration would be made by HALO (high altitude, low opening) from twelve thousand feet. Karpov assured the general that all Spetsnaz team members were HALO proficient. Once on the ground, actions would be designated by the situation. Mattson would be in charge of the Americans, Karpov would command the Spetsnaz. B.J. would handle the rounding up of the SOCOM personnel and their transportation to MacDill and Panama. Secretary Bowers would return to Washington to keep the president advised of the mission's progress.

It was 0530 when General Johnson and the others boarded the plane. Colonel Karpov hesitated on the steps. Turning to B.J., he said, "I am looking forward to working with you, Major Mattson. Let's hope that together, we can get them all out, unharmed." He extended his hand.

B.J. didn't hesitate this time. The Russian's grip was firm and his words sounded sincere. In the three and a half hours since they had met, Mattson had learned to appreciate the man for his professionalism and honest concern for the situation. Both men realized that they cared for their commanders more than either would admit. If the other Russian members of the team were anything like Karpov, there should be no problems.

"Me, too, Colonel. We'll give it our best shot. See you in Panama tonight."

Karpov waved a final time as he knelt down inside the aircraft, retracted the steps, and shut the door. Out on the runway, Mattson watched the jet streak down the strip and lift off into the blackness, only seconds ahead of the predawn gray of the morning, which was beginning to edge its way along the horizon. B.J. watched the plane until its flashing strobe lights were out of sight. He did not linger long. It was going to be a long day and there was plenty to be done. Swinging into the jeep, he headed for the main gate entrance to hangar 3. There he saw his first problem of the morning.

Two Air Force security men had General Sweet spread-eagled against the chain link fence. Mattson was tempted to turn around, take the long way around the hangar, and leave Sweet to experience firsthand the expertise of the "over-dressed, rent-a-cops," a term the general had often used to describe the Air Force's crack security unit. It appeared that the two airmen shaking the general down had heard of the man's opinion of them. Sweet was getting the full treatment normally reserved for a terrorist. A third security man stood off to the side with his rifle leveled at Sweet. All three looked back at

B.J. as he stepped out of the jeep and walked toward the fence. They were grinning, loving every minute of this.

Sweet was rattling off a line of verbal abuse and screaming, "I'm a goddamn general, you idiots. Can't you fucking see that?"

The young sergeant holding the rifle replied, "Sorry, sir, but when you were refused entry, you shouldn't have tried to push your way past the sentries. We were instructed to keep everyone out, sir. Your name wasn't on any special exceptions list. We sure wouldn't have wanted to ruin our 'rent-a-cop' reputation by breaking the rules, now would we?"

"You young smart ass! I'll have your—" For the first time, Sweet noticed Mattson standing behind him.

"Problem, General?" asked B.J. innocently.

"Major! Thank God! Will you please tell these idiots who the hell I am?"

A host of possibilities came to mind: asshole, Judas, brownnoser, and Pentagon spy, but B.J. had no time to discuss the general's finer points. He had too much to do to play games with Sweet. "Sergeant, this man is General Sweet. He is with the SOCOM Command."

The sergeant saluted as he replied, "Thank you, sir. We thought that was who he was, but his attitude really sucked, so we thought we had better check him out. Since you are preparing to leave, Major, am I clear to give a stand down order to my people around the perimeter?"

"Yes, and thank you for your help, Sergeant."

Glancing over at the frustrated general, who was trying to straighten his uniform and still muttering under his breath, the airman whispered, "Believe me, Major, it was our pleasure. Good day, sir."

By the time Sweet got himself together, the three airmen were driving off. He started to yell for them to stop. He wanted their names. Mattson interrupted him. "Can I offer you a ride back to headquarters, General?"

Sweet's face was beet red. It was hard to tell if it was from rage or pure embarrassment, or both.

"No, Major! I have my vehicle here. Where is General Johnson? And who was on that plane? Why all the security?"

Mattson walked back to his jeep and slid in behind the wheel as he answered, "Secretary of defense, sir. He and the general are old friends from way back. Guess they decided to do a little flying today. Nothing special about the security, sir. These Air Force 'rent-a-cops' really are pretty good, wouldn't you say? Well, got to go, General. See you later." Mattson snapped off a salute and drove away. He had a lot of phone calls to make, but then, so did General Sweet.

CHAPTER 7

Naval Special Warfare Center
Coronado, California

Lieutenant Commander Jake Mortimer dropped down on the front steps of the instructors' office and lowered his head on his sweat covered arms. He had just finished a grueling seven mile run through the ankle-deep sand along the beach. In a way, he would regret having to return to Florida. The past week had been both informative and entertaining. The new underwater laser weapons had developed testing problems the third day into their trial run, but once the bugs had been worked out, they would enhance the SEALs' already impressive arsenal and move them one step closer to the capability of fighting wars that had only been imagined by science fiction writers a few short years ago.

One of the SEAL instructors stuck his head out the door. "Commander Mortimer, sir, you have a phone call. Major Mattson from MacDill. You can take it in the CO's office, sir."

Jake stood. A sudden twinge of pain shot down the back of his legs, reminding him that he had not used the proper cool down procedures required following such a run. Thanking the instructor, Jake went into the office and picked up the phone. Not wanting to leave sweat stains on the chief instructor's

96

chair, he sat on the edge of the windowsill. "Hey, B.J., what's shakin' down Florida way?"

"Our boy, Sweet," came the reply.

"What?" laughed Jake.

"Never mind. Listen, Jake. We've got a hot situation on our hands. I've got a list of names in front of me. Two of them are Navy SEALs who are stationed there at Coronado. Do you know a Lieutenant Commander Hatcher McGee and a Chief Petty Officer Jimmy Mitchell?"

Jake was on his feet now. The thought of getting back into action had already started the adrenaline flowing. The two names B.J. had just mentioned indicated that whatever the mission, SOCOM was handpicking the best.

Hatcher McGee had been Jake's first SEAL team commander in those early days of his chosen profession. McGee was a bear of a man who stood six foot four and weighed 230 pounds of solid muscle. The sheer size of the man suggested a certain amount of clumsiness, yet Jake had never met a man of Hatcher's size so quick with his hands and feet. This was demonstrated by his ability to stand flat-footed in the center of a room, leap straight up, and kick high enough to shatter a light bulb in the ceiling. In the water, he was even more agile. He was a man totally oblivious to fear, an attitude evolved from five years in Vietnam, two of which were spent as a POW at the famed Hanoi Hilton. McGee seldom ran without a T-shirt to cover the scars from the beatings he had received in captivity. It was an ordeal that he rarely discussed with anyone, and then only in sentences of five words or less.

The second name, Chief Jimmy Mitchell, meant there was going to be jungle work involved. Mitchell was another impressive hunk; six-two, with arms that were larger than most men's legs. His massive chest encased rippling muscles that could win the man a Mr. America title any time he wanted to bother to try for it. Mitch, as he was known to his friends, was an expert tracker and an all-around Tarzan when it came to jungle work. Jake had been curious as to why a man who liked the jungle so much wasn't in the Rangers or the Green Berets instead of being a Navy SEAL. The answer Mitch had given him hadn't been what he had expected from a man big enough to tear a grizzly bear apart with his bare hands. It was the water. Mitch loved the perfect silence, the beauty and serenity of the depths of the sea.

Wait a minute, thought Jake. There's only one other man here who knows the jungle better than Mitchell—Hatcher! He was a natural. His mother and father had been archaeologists studying ancient ruins in South America. Hatcher McGee had spent the first eighteen years of his life in Brazil, the country in which he had been born.

"Jake, you still with me?" asked B.J.

Mortimer grinned and replied, "Sure thing, B.J. When do we hit the jungles of Brazil?"

There was a stunned silence. Then B.J. asked, "How in the hell did you know that?"

Jake laughed as he replied, "Guess I've just been hanging around with you too long, B.J. All that intelligence office shit is starting to rub off on me."

"Well, good. That means all my work hasn't been for nothing. Are McGee and Mitchell still there?"

"Yeah. Hatcher is out on one of the islands playing guerrilla chief for a final exercise and Mitchell just finished trying to run me and a batch of new candidates into our first heart attack. He got four rings on the bell five minutes after we finished the run."

The bell Jake referred to was an ancient mariners' ship bell that hung on the wall beside the instructors' door. Each new candidate who volunteered for SEAL training had been provided with a round-trip ticket to the island. As they were all volunteers, any one of them could quit the course whenever they figured they'd had enough. A candidate only had to step up to the bell and ring it once and they were out of there.

B.J. was about to say something when he heard the clear clang of the bell in the background as another volunteer decided the SEAL business wasn't for him.

"Make it five," amended Jake.

"Yeah, I heard that one. Listen, Jake, I need you, McGee, and Mitchell back here no later than 1600 hours today. I've made arrangements with San Diego Naval Air Station. They'll have a special flight waiting for you. Show time is 1000 hours. Any problem with making that, Jake?" asked B.J.

Jimmy Mitchell walked into the office and grabbed a can of V-8 juice from the icebox in the corner.

Jake looked at him as he answered B.J.'s question. "No problem, boss. San Diego, 1000 hours. Me, McGee, and Mitchell. Hey, B.J., I hope this doesn't have anything to do with that little captain with the cute ass we have down there."

Mitchell's eyebrows lifted. Whatever it was, he liked it already.

Mattson paused before he answered. Jake and Pat Longly had dated a couple of times before she left for Brazil. Jake was very fond of her.

"Afraid it does, partner. She's in some deep shit. She, her team, and a Russian colonel."

Jake almost fell over the desk. "A what?"

"Fill you in later, Jake. Gotta go. See you at 1600 this afternoon. Bye."

"Roger. Out," said Jake as he hung up the phone and turned to Mitchell. "You ready to do some rockin' and rollin', Mitch?"

Downing the V-8 in one gulp, Mitchell smiled. "Hell yes, Commander, I just had a V-8."

"Well, go pack your shit. We're out of here. As soon as I get back from the island with Hatcher, we'll be heading for MacDill."

Mitchell crumpled the can into a piece of metal no larger than a half dollar and tossed it into the trash can. Walking out the door, he came face to face with a sweat-soaked and weary looking candidate who held his hand suspended only inches from the bell rope. Smiling as he moved down the steps, Mitch said, "You might want to think about that, kid. I just got orders outta here. No tellin' when I'll be back—might be weeks."

The young Navy volunteer managed to force a slight smile on his exhausted face. "No—no kidding, chief?"

"I wouldn't shit you, candidate. I'm really gonna miss these early morning runs. See you around, kid," said Mitchell as he stepped off into the sand and headed for his quarters.

The candidate watched in silence as his worst nightmare

walked away. Pulling his hand back from the rope as if it were a white-hot poker, he dropped to his knees in the sand. "Thank God!" he whispered.

0630 (EST)—June 22
Ranger Headquarters
Fort Benning, Georgia

"Headquarters—2nd Ranger Battalion, 75th Rangers. Sergeant Major Adams speaking, sir," said Jack Adams as he cradled the phone against his shoulder while pouring himself a cup of coffee.

"Hey, Snake! How's it hanging?"

Adams stood holding the coffeepot and the cup suspended in midair. He recognized the voice immediately. He set the pot down, relaxed back in his chair, and jokingly said, "I'm sorry, sir. This line is reserved for ten-fingered officers only. If you want, I can give you the handicapped number."

B.J. was laughing as he replied, "Boy, you're still a cold-hearted bitch in the mornings, Snake."

"You're just lucky you caught me in a good mood. B.J., how the hell you doing? Tell me you're on post."

"No such luck, Jack—MacDill. Look here, Snake, your name came up on a computer readout as an area specialist on South America—the Amazon Basin of Brazil, in particular. Could you give me a little background on that, Jack?"

Adams took a sip of his coffee, allowing the gaze from his light brown eyes to drift up the wall to a framed photo next to his desk. Four camouflaged men sat on the deck of a UH1H helicopter. Kneeling in front of them were six Brazilian commandos. All the men in the picture were in full combat gear with Car-15 rifles. A much younger Sergeant First Class Jack Adams sat in the middle of the group. This had been the team that had tracked down Castro's top guerrilla leaders in the jungles of the Amazon Basin ten years ago. Stretching his wiry, long and lanky six-foot frame until his boots rested comfortably on top of his desk, he leaned back in the chair and related the story of his Brazilian adventure. When he had finished, he said, "B.J., if you got something going down, I'd really appreciate it if you'd let me in on it. This damn paperwork around here is going to put me in an old soldiers' home before my time. I could sure use a break."

Mattson was silent for a moment, then asked, "Jack, do you think you can handle it down there?"

Adams's legs recoiled off the desk as he sat straight up in his chair. B.J. was politely trying to tell him he might be too old for another romp through the jungle. Hell, he was only forty-nine, and for a man with four tours of Vietnam and eighteen years in the Green Berets, with another six in the Rangers, he was just beginning to reach his stride.

"Sonny! You just tell me when and where, then get out of the way," said Jack.

"Okay," chuckled B.J., "as long as you don't need to carry a pacemaker, I guess you'll do."

"Now, who's being cold-hearted, you prick!"

Mattson laughed again and asked, "Jack, you've also got a Sergeant First Class Roy Fletcher down there who's on my list. From the information I have, he's a top-line medic with plenty of jungle experience. You know him?"

"You just restored my faith in computers, B.J. Fletcher's probably the best damn doctor in the country practicing without a license. Flew chase medic in the twilight days of the Southeast Asian war games. Was shot down three times. Silver Star for Grenada, and should have gotten another one for the Panama invasion. Kept one amputee and sucking chest wounds alive through the night until he could get them out at daylight. Anybody better than this guy is already working at the Mayo Clinic."

"That sounds like our man. Okay, Jack, I'll fax special orders for both of you. I need you here no later than 1600 hours. You remember Master Sergeant Tommy Smith, Special Operations Wing?"

"Yeah—Smitty. Haven't seen him in a while."

"He's just across the river from you at Fort Rucker. Special arrangements will be made to fly all three of you to MacDill. You contact Fletcher and I'll alert Smith to be waiting for you. Plan to be at the airfield by 1100 hours. And, Jack, carry light—we'll be in Panama by 2100 tonight."

Jack Adams suddenly became serious as he said, "Thanks, B.J."

"For what?" asked Mattson.

"For making an old man feel like he's still needed."

"Hope you still feel the same way later, Jack. It could get nasty real quick."

"Wouldn't want it any other way. See you soon, B.J. Bye."

General Sweet came down the hallway and stopped in the doorway of Mattson's office just as B.J. was hanging up the phone. The little man's face was flushed. Mattson could see the veins in the general's chubby neck pulsating. He didn't speak, but rather stared at Mattson with his small beady eyes that seemed to glow with malice. "Something I can do for you, General?" asked Mattson respectfully.

Sweet's hands balled into twin fists, his knuckles showing white. In a slow, sarcastic voice, he uttered, "Someday, Major, someday." His threat made, Sweet pivoted on his heel, stormed off to his office, and slammed the door.

"Yeah—well, this ain't the day, General!" said B. J. Mattson as he began making a list of the logistical requirements for the upcoming mission.

0730 hours
General Garland's office
The Pentagon

General John Garland listened patiently as Sweet ranted on about the way he had been treated, while at the same time apologizing for not having secured the information Garland had wanted. Garland waited until he thought Sweet had nearly exhausted himself, then said, "Raymond, that's all right. Our friend Mr. Burrows at the National Security Council was able to provide us with the information we needed."

"Good, John," exclaimed Sweet. "How in the hell are we going to nail these bastards?"

Garland's answer was not what the little general had expected. "We're not, Raymond. This one, we've decided to stay out of the way. Too many people in high places are going to be watching every step of their operation this time. All we can do is hope they screw it up themselves."

The disappointment was obvious in Sweet's voice as he stammered, "But—but, John, they humiliated me in front of—"

Garland cut him off. "Forget that, Raymond. Do you remember the last time you were here? You stated that you had not been able to place SOCOM in the compromising situations we had hoped for because it was more than one man could handle and you asked us for help."

"Yes, sir. That was just before that Chad business. I still say the same thing. I need someone else to work with me."

"Well, Mr. Burrows believes he has found us just the man for that little job. I want you to come to Washington tonight. I think you should meet your new associate as soon as possible."

Sweet was ecstatic. At last he was going to have someone on his side. "Yes, sir, I'll be there tonight."

"Fine, Raymond. See you then. Good-bye."

"Good-bye, sir—and thank you."

Leaning forward to replace the receiver, Sweet saw Major Mattson pass the doorway, whistling as he went down the hall. Folding his hands on his desk, the general whispered to himself, "Go ahead, Major. Enjoy yourself while you can. I can't touch you on this one, but next time it will be different. My day is coming, and before it's over, I'll have your ass hanging on my wall as a souvenir of what happens to smart-asses who mess with Raymond Sweet."

1300 hours—June 22
Medina estate
Colombia

Patrica Longly placed her hand on Colonel Molotov's forehead. The man was burning with fever. He had been fading in and out of consciousness ever since the shooting. The wound to his shoulder had been a clear in and out shot. No bones had been hit, and damage at the exit hole had been minimal. However, Arias's sadistic shot to his knee had caused devastating damage. Half of his kneecap had been blown away. The impact splintered the tips of the upper and lower leg bones.

Muscle and tissue trauma were extensive. It was beyond Patrica Longly's imagination how anyone could stand the pain of such a wound. Yet, during his periods of consciousness, the man Arias had called a Russian spoke coherently, as if the shattered leg were not even a part of his body and the pain was nonexistent.

Rinsing a rag in the bucket of water that had been provided for the captives, she placed it on his forehead and leaned back on her heels.

Sergeant Watson came over and knelt down beside her. "How is he doing?" he asked.

Longly glanced down at the crude bandage they had fashioned from part of Watson's T-shirt. Arias had spirited them away from the site of the killings so fast that their medical bags had been left in the van. By the time Longly had convinced Arias that they were going to need them, it was too late. The commander of the Brazilian soldiers had ordered the van set afire. They would blame the destruction of the van and the disappearance of its passengers on the terrorists.

"We have to convince these people that we need morphine sulfate, saline, and instruments to work on this man. Otherwise, he is going to die. Look at this place," said the captain, waving her hand to the side to indicate the dirt floor and corrugated tin shed that had become their prison. "Infection has already begun to set in around the wound. Even with the best medical attention, I doubt we could save his leg."

Watson stared down at the blood-soaked bandage. He knew she was right. Her hand reached over and gently touched the swollen, discolored spot where Arias had kicked him. "How are you doing, Sergeant?" she asked.

It hurt like hell, and at times his vision blurred for no apparent reason, but he wasn't about to tell her that. Young Captain Longly already had enough on her mind. "Awh, it ain't nothing, Captain. Ma used to bop us kids harder than that wimp did."

Looking down at the elderly man lying in front of him, Watson asked, "Captain, you got any idea who this guy is and what the hell is going on?"

Brushing a wisp of hair from in front of her eyes, she

replied, "No, Sergeant. All I know is this man and the one killed outside the van are supposed to be Russians, and they did something to a man called Medina. They seem to think whatever it was, we're somehow involved." Longly's voice trailed off as she softly said, "Poor Sergeant Foley. I—I wish there had been something I could have done to—to—"

Watson wrapped a strong arm around her small shoulders and pulled her to him. "No, Captain. There was nothing you or any of us could've done. Don't you be blamin' yourself for that. We're gonna get out of here, believe me. Once ol' Q-Tip hears 'bout this, you better believe he'll scramble SOCOM and come ridin' in here like the cavalry to the rescue. Besides, you was datin' Commander Mortimer 'fore we left, wasn't you?"

Turning her tearstained eyes up to the black sergeant, she nodded that she was.

"Well, hell then, we're as good as outta here. The general'll have the M & M boys down here so fast, this guy Medina will be wishin' he'd never seen an American before. So, you don't worry, okay? We'll be outta here real soon."

Longly had gained strength from the man's words. The thought of Jake coming to her rescue sent a warm feeling through her. She really cared for him. Looking across the room at Sergeants Cochran and Foster as they slept against one of the walls, she prayed Jake would hurry. She did not want to see anyone else die. "Thank you, Sergeant Watson, I—"

The door suddenly swung open. Two gunmen walked in, followed by Arias and a fat man she had not seen before. Watson and Longly stood up as the men approached Molotov.

"Is he dead?" asked the fat man.

The captain could feel the fat man's eyes staring at her breasts. "No, not yet. But he will be, if you don't give us something to help him."

Arias stepped forward to survey his work. His boot lashed out, striking Molotov just below the wounded knee. Longly was grateful that the man was unconscious.

"Stop that, you animal!" she screamed.

Her voice woke Foster and Cochran who jumped to their

feet, only to have four of Medina's men step in through the door and level their guns at them.

Arias looked at her, then to Medina. "We should go ahead and kill them all now," he said. "All except the bitch, of course. She has fire. Fucking her would be highly entertaining, I would think."

Watson turned on Arias. "You scumbag bastard. You touch her, and I'll kill your ass."

Arias laughed. "You silly black fool. I see now why the gringos call you niggers. Your ignorance is unbelievable." Arias's hand shot out so fast that it surprised Watson. The slap sent him back against the tin wall. Two men quickly grabbed Watson's arms, and Arias hit him again.

"Enough, Rodrigo!" shouted Medina.

The men released Watson while Arias returned to the fat man's side.

Medina, his eyes still taking in the full beauty of the woman, asked, "Would you please compile a list of the necessary medical supplies that you need, and I will see that they are brought to you."

Longly was surprised by the man's gentle tone of voice. It seemed so out of place, considering the ruthless men standing around him. "Thank you—Mr.—Mr.—"

"Carlos Medina, Captain. I regret that you and your friends have become pawns in a complicated matter involving our friend, Colonel Molotov, whom you seem so concerned about. Let's hope the ordeal will soon be over, and you and the others will be free to go. In the meantime, I am afraid these quarters are the best I can offer you. Security reasons—I'm sure you can understand. I will send one of my men for the list within the hour. Until then, I bid you good day. Come, Arias."

After the men had departed, Foster and Cochran helped Watson to his feet.

Longly brought a pen and paper from the cargo pocket of her fatigues and began working on the list.

Seeing the captain concentrating on her work, Watson pulled the other two men to a corner of the room. Wiping the blood from his split lip, he whispered, "We're gettin' the hell outta here tonight. Be ready."

1630 hours—June 22
Hangar 3
MacDill AFB

"Excuse me all to hell, Major, but you got to be out of your fuckin' mind!" growled Hatcher McGee after Mattson had informed the newly arrived group of the planned joint operation. "Bad enough thinking of working with Russians any time, but the Spetsnaz! Jesus, Major Mattson, those are the guys who killed every man and woman in the presidential palace in Kabul, the night the Russians invaded Afghanistan. Trained the damn NVA in Hanoi during 'Nam, especially the Vietnamese interrogators. Now we're supposed to work side by side with 'em like none of that ever happened. You got a lot of balls, Major, I'll give you that."

Adams, Fletcher, Mitchell, Smith, and Jake all sat silently listening to Hatcher's objection to the operation. They all knew he had been a prisoner of war. It was easy to understand his bitterness. B.J. knew this as well. However, from reading McGee's record, Mattson felt that McGee was professional enough to put aside personal differences and dislikes for a mission's sake.

"Commander McGee," said B.J. after the big man had sat down, "times change and with them, the way people think. The world is entering a new era of understanding. We can either join in this change or dwell in the past. Myself, I welcome any change that might possibly turn an enemy into an ally. I cannot, nor will I try, to argue the points you have made. I can, however, assure you that this mission is going forward—with or without you. I chose you, Commander, because of your background and knowledge of the area in question. It goes without saying that such knowledge would provide the mission with a distinct advantage. Somewhere down there in those jungles is an American captain and what's left of her medical team. We don't know what they're doing to her at this minute. I don't like to think about that. I will, however, venture to say that I am certain Captain Longly could care less if her rescuers are American or Russian. The decision is yours, Commander." Looking to the others of the group, Mattson said, "That goes for the rest of you, as well. This mission will be launched, no matter who goes or who stays. Those who are going, put your bags on the plane. We're taking off for Panama in thirty minutes. Jake, you get 'em squared away. I have to contact the old man and give him our departure time. When I get back, we're out of here."

Mitchell stood beside Jake and whispered, "The major was kinda hard on Hatch, wasn't he?"

"Maybe so, Mitch, but I've worked with B.J. for a while now. There's a reason behind everything he does. I think he just wanted to put the operation in the proper perspective for Commander McGee."

Mitchell nodded and said, "Yeah. The bottom line is, our people are in trouble and need our help, no matter what it takes, right?"

Jake smiled and slapped the big Navy man on the back. "You got it. Let's load our stuff on board and see if we can find us a window seat. B.J. said the Russians cleared it with Castro for us to fly straight over Cuba for Panama. I'd kind of like to see what the place looks like from the air."

Mitchell grabbed up his bag and followed Jake to the plane. The others followed suit. Sergeant Major Adams paused as he walked past McGee. He could understand the Navy commander's bitterness, but he could only imagine the nightmare of being tortured day and night by men who had been taught their trade by Soviet experts, namely the Spetsnaz. Adams could see clearly the soul-searching on McGee's face. He started to say something, then thought better of it. Like B.J. had said, it was a decision only McGee could make.

B.J. returned to the hangar. General Johnson had already cleared their arrival and the arrival of the Russian team with the Southern Command and Howard Air Force Base. As had been done here, a special area and hangar were cordoned off and security was at its maximum. Soviet intelligence, with the cooperation of Cuban agents in Colombia, had verified that the captives were being held at Medina's estate near the Colombian border with Brazil. Walking to the plane, B.J. saw McGee was the only man still sitting in one of the seven chairs in front of the podium. His instincts must have been wrong. So be it.

McGee heard the footsteps of Mattson's boots on the concrete as he made his way to the ladder leading up to the cabin of the sleek, air-conditioned, executive jet with the Philco-Ford emblem on its sides. Mattson paused at the first step to look back at McGee one last time. The big man only stared at him. He didn't move. The pilots already had the engines running as Mattson entered the cool atmosphere of the cabin and found himself a seat next to a window.

The crew chief walked by, knelt down, and reached out to pull in the ladder. "Hold it, Chief," said Tommy Smith with a grin. The others turned in their seats, looking to the rear of the plane. "Looks like we got one more passenger."

2000 hours—June 22
Howard AFB
Panama

The jet banked left over the small mountains surrounding the picturesque air base with its runway lights aglow. Beyond the hills were the lights of Panama City, ablaze with its people enjoying the city's newfound freedom from the pock-faced general who had suppressed them for so long. McGee sat alone at the back of the plane. He hadn't spoken since coming aboard. That worried Mattson. He had to know they could depend on the man if this was going to work.

The wheels touched down and the pilots taxied toward the designated hangar. The ring of Air Force security guards opened ranks to allow the plane to enter, then they smoothly flowed back into the gap. B.J. saw General Johnson, Ballock, and Yelintikov standing near a briefing area that had been set up in one corner of the hangar. Behind them stood Colonel Karpov and his team of Spetsnaz, wearing their traditional blue-and-white-striped T-shirts beneath their camouflage jungle shirts and their powder blue berets atop their heads. Everyone on the team was staring at the Russians, all but McGee.

The ladder came down, and Johnson walked up to greet the men. Taking the team to the briefing area, the general introduced Mr. Ballock and Yelintikov. The Americans eyed the Russian with the bushy eyebrows closely as they shook his hand. They had already figured Ballock for an agency man. Then came the introductions that they were more interested in. These, General Johnson turned over to the team's commander. Colonel Karpov called the group to attention. Their heels snapped in unison as their leader walked to the end of the line and began calling out their names. They were all big men and appeared in excellent physical condition. Their ages ranged from the early twenties to the mid-thirties, with Karpov being the oldest at age forty-four.

"Major Boris Suslov, my executive officer." The officer took one step forward and slapped his heels together.

Karpov continued, each man stepping forward as his name was called.

"Lieutenant Alexi Chivenov, my medical officer.

"Sergeant Alexander Trotsky, team leader and demolitions specialist.

"Sergeant Grigori Kerenski, weapons specialist.

"Sergeant Leonid Zhukov, jungle warfare expert and tracker.

"Sergeant Issak Gorki, communications specialist.

"And I, gentlemen, am Colonel Alexei Karpov, commander of this detachment. I would like at this time to say that my men and I are looking forward to working with you all."

General Johnson thanked the colonel, then had Mattson introduce his team. B.J., forgoing the formal introduction of his counterpart, casually named each of the Americans and their areas of expertise. McGee was mentioned last.

As Mattson finished, McGee added a last line to B.J.'s introduction. "And former prisoner of the North Vietnamese for two years!"

There was no mistaking the sarcasm in Hatcher McGee's voice. It was clear that the remark bothered Johnson and Yelintikov.

Colonel Karpov, in typical fashion, showed no expression, choosing to ignore the remark. He said, "General, I would suggest we begin. All members of my team are fluent in English. Therefore, please feel free to conduct your briefing at whatever rate is comfortable to you."

"Thank you, and that's a good idea, Colonel," said Johnson. "Gentlemen, if you will take your seats, we'll get started."

In theory, the plan for this joint operation had seemed simple enough. Two teams of professional soldiers from separate countries, equally well trained, with only one goal to achieve, the rescue of imprisoned comrades. It quickly became apparent that the only simple thing about this operation was going to be the actual combat itself. Inadvertently, the chairs placed in front of the briefing charts had been arranged in two rows of seven each. Karpov and the Spetsnaz filled in the first row, leaving Mattson and the Americans to sit behind the Russians. Neither B.J. nor the others thought anything of it at the moment, but for McGee it somehow seemed to imply that they were second best.

Picking up his chair, Hatcher moved it forward and to the left of Karpov. Adams, then Mitchell, did the same, with the others following suit until there no longer was a second row—only one long line in front of the podium. It seemed a minor thing, but to General Johnson it indicated that for all the smiles and formal protocol, the bitterness between these two forces was not going to be reconciled by one mission. If anything, this simple act demonstrated the potential for disaster. Yelintikov realized this as well, yet there was little that could be done about it now. Each minute that ticked away on the clock brought the execution of Molotov closer to reality. The two leaders could only hope that the group assembled before them could put aside their personal differences and, once in the target area, function as the fine-tuned fighting machines they were, having only a single thought among them, the rescue of the captives.

General Johnson waited until the seating arrangements had been completed to everyone's satisfaction, with Jake being the last member of the group to move his chair on line. The look he was receiving from Q-Tip was a combination of irritation crossed with concern.

When Johnson flipped the cover off the first set of charts to his right, the team found themselves staring at an enlarged aerial photo that had been taken by an American spy satellite only hours before. It centered on the border area between

Colombia and Brazil. Dense jungle and rain forests were prevalent, flanked on either side by two small bodies of water that were tributaries of the Amazon River. Located in the middle of this vast jungle was an area approximately one mile in diameter that had been cleared, showing fences, corrals, and a number of outbuildings, surrounding a large two-story mansion that sat in the very center of the clearing—the Medina estate.

Johnson began by explaining why the Colombian government, which had joined with the United States in the crackdown on drugs, could not simply mount their own raid on the well-known mansion shown in the photo. Medina's former employer, Petratina, had been a highly intelligent man before becoming addicted to cocaine. He had taken advantage of an age-old feud that had developed between Colombia and Brazil, a dispute over a twenty-mile-wide strip of land that separated the two countries. Each side declared that the land was theirs. It was here that Petratina had cleared the land and built his drug empire, complete with airstrips. By bankrolling high officials in the Brazilian government, he assured himself protection from interference by Colombian officials and their armies. Any incursion into the disputed zone would be considered an act of aggression by the Brazilian government and would constitute a declaration of war between the two nations. The matter of legal ownership had been before the international world courts for over twenty years and still no decision had been handed down as to who actually owned the land in question. As long as Medina, like his predecessor, continued his payoffs to those who held the controlling votes in the court, there would never be a final verdict.

Combining intelligence reports from the CIA, the Russian GRU, and Cuban agents in Colombia, they had placed Medina's total, full-time strength at the estate at 80 men. That number usually increased from 80 to 150 during actual drug transactions, which normally occurred three days a week. Armament for the drug soldiers consisted of AK-47s, M-16s, M203 40mm grenade launchers, and a variety of the Heckler and Koch range of 9mm submachine guns. Three M-60 machine guns were clearly visible atop the house itself.

Stepping to the photo, Johnson drew a large red circle around a tin shack that sat a hundred yards from the main house. This was where the agents reported the prisoners were being held.

Brian Ballock moved along the line of volunteers, passing out eight-by-tens of the photos the general had on his briefing easel, making it easier for the men to follow his remarks. Flipping to another aerial photo that began at the far left of the previous one, he indicated that the photos had been taken moving east to west. This one covered an area approximately three miles square and consisted of nothing but massive jungle, hills, and the occasional appearance of a river snaking its way beneath openings in the rain forest. There were no clearings or openings that could be utilized for drop zones. It was going to have to be a rough terrain jump. Each man would carry a hundred-foot rope. Once landing in the treetops, they would rappel to the ground and link up for movement to the target area. Johnson faced the group and said, "If anyone is injured during this insertion, that individual or individuals will be moved to an area that provides adequate cover and conceal-ment. Medical personnel will provide whatever immediate attention is possible and be sure that sufficient painkillers are left with the injured. No one! And I mean no one will remain with the injured. They will be recovered following the com-pletion of the operation. Is that clear?" asked Johnson.

The line of professionals all nodded. Flipping to the next picture, the general touched his pointer to the photo of the joint CIA/DEA airstrip and camp that was located 250 miles east of Bogotá. It reminded Mattson of the A-camps they had estab-lished during the Vietnam era, complete with bunkers, barbed wire, and lookout towers. At one end of the long runway sat an unmarked C-130 transport plane. Two Blackhawk helicopters were on the left of the runway. Next to them and farther down were three Cobra gunships, and across the runaway sat four UH1H Huey model helicopters, the old workhorse of the Vietnam War.

The team would depart Panama for this base, code named Blue Boy, where they would be outfitted for the mission. The Medina estate lay 120 miles due east of Blue Boy. Flying time to the target would be one hour. Everything on the logistical lists that had been requested by Mattson and Karpov had already been flown to the base and was waiting for them. Master Sergeant Tommy Smith would remain at Blue Boy to organize the chopper crews for the extraction of the team following the raid, as well as to handle any on-call requests for close air-ground support during the mission and extraction.

Placing the pointer on the podium, Johnson put his hands on his hips and said, "That's it, gentlemen. The Colombian government has not been informed of your intentions for obvious security reasons. The drug cartel has informants everywhere. Once you are on the ground, you're on your own. Are there any questions?"

Colonel Karpov stood and asked, "Comrade General, should we need air support during the night, will your pilots at this base be utilizing the PVS night-vision system?"

"Yes, Colonel. They have extensive training in that field and of course they will be under the direction of Master Sergeant Smith at all times."

"Thank you, sir," said Karpov, who sat back down.

"Any other questions, gentlemen?" asked Johnson, pausing for a moment. "Okay, fine. Gentlemen, this operation is the first of its kind ever to be attempted by our two countries. Things of the past belong in the past. It is a new era that has quickly advanced upon us. Changes are occurring all over our planet that will rewrite history and alter the maps of the world as we know it. We can and must face this new progress together—for time waits for no man. I hope this operation will be remembered as the spark that ignited a new understanding between the two most powerful countries in the world. I can only say that there is more at stake here than just the rescue of our prisoners. I am sure you all know what I mean by that. I wish you all luck and Godspeed." Looking to Yelintikov, the general asked, "Would you care to say something, sir?"

Yelintikov shook his head and replied, "No, General, I believe you have put the situation in its proper perspective better than I could. I would only add my own wishes for your success, gentlemen."

"Okay, then, that's it. You will depart for Blue Boy in thirty minutes. Mr. Yelintikov and I will be flying to our embassies in Bogotá, where we will monitor your progress and relay that information to Washington and the Kremlin. Mr. Ballock will monitor from Blue Boy. Once again, good luck!"

Colonel Karpov yelled, "Attention!" in English.

Both teams came straight out of their chairs, snapping to attention as B.J. and Karpov saluted the departing commander.

Waiting until the general had cleared the hangar doors, B.J. shouted, "At ease!"

Some of the men gathered around the large picture of Blue Boy that still remained on the easel.

Sergeant First Class Roy "Doc" Fletcher came up to Mattson. "Sir, I just wanted you to know how much I appreciate you letting me in on this. Snake Adams floored me when he called and said he had orders for both of us. Minute I found out I was going to be workin' with you and Jake Mortimer I knew it was going to be a good one, but I would have never guessed I'd be working with the Russians."

"Does it bother you, Doc?" asked B.J.

The tall, rangy man from North Carolina smiled. Although only in his mid-thirties, Doc Fletcher had soft streaks of silver running through his light brown hair. The blue-green eyes sparkled as he talked.

"Hell no, Major, I'm one of those Southern boys that can get along with anybody. Especially when I know I'm going to be puttin' my ass in their hands."

Mattson laughed as Jake joined them.

Seeing the Russian medical officer, Lieutenant Chivenov, standing by himself near the charts, Doc said, "Well, if you all will excuse me, I'd kinda like to talk shop with their head medicine man."

Jake and B.J. nodded their approval as Fletcher went over and shook hands with the officer. Within minutes they were both laughing.

"Wish we could spread a little of Doc's attitude around these other guys," said B.J.

"I heard that," replied Jake, as he stared across the hangar at Hatcher McGee, who stood alone near the hangar doors, looking up at the night sky. "I can't really blame Hatch for the way he feels, B.J. Those two years as a POW took a lot out of him. I don't mean physically—God, the man's harder than a keg of bent nails—but I mean inside. There's a lot of bitterness in there. Bitterness and resentment that needs to be released. It's been eating him up for years. But he wouldn't let anyone get close enough to him to help him deal with it. Hell, I was on his team for a year before I even knew he'd been a POW. He hides it pretty well. I think if you would have told him the Russians were going to be involved, he wouldn't have come. Some memories are just too painful."

Mattson looked down at his hand with the missing finger. He knew all about bitterness and resentment. It was a Russian AK that had shattered his hand and destroyed his dreams of ever being a surgeon. But like the general said, times were changing faster than anyone had ever imagined possible. The past belonged in the past. Hatcher would have to work it out with himself. B.J. had.

Mitchell came up to the group. Sergeant Zhukov, the Spetsnaz jungle expert and tracker, was with him. Mitchell slapped the Russian on the back and smiled at B.J. and Jake. "You know, if I didn't know any better, I'd swear me and Leonid here went to the same damn jungle schools. The guy's good. Textbook perfect and then some."

Mattson grinned. "You'll find there isn't a hell of a lot of difference between men in this profession, Mitch. Only different uniforms and patches."

Pointing to a soda machine in the corner, Mitchell kept his arm around Zhukov as he said, "Come on, Leonid, I'll buy you a Pepsi."

The Russian's eyes lit up. "Oh, yeah. Is that the one they advertise by setting Michael Jackson's hair on fire?"

"Something like that. Come on, I'll tell you about how that happened," laughed Mitchell as he led the man off toward the machine.

B.J. looked around the hangar to see what the other members of the team were doing and how they were getting along. Tommy Smith, Snake Adams, Karpov, and his executive officer, Major Suslov were still discussing the area around Medina's estate. Smith was making gestures with his hand, demonstrating how he would bring in the choppers in different situations, should they be needed.

Sergeants Trotsky and Gorki, seeing Mitchell and Zhukov at the Pepsi machine, were crossing the hangar to join them. Everyone was involved and making an effort to ease the tensions of earlier; all but McGee, who still remained apart from the group, satisfied to be left alone. That bothered Mattson. He considered leaving the man here. It could save them problems later. Yet McGee was the only man in the room that had enough extensive knowledge of the country and terrain. He knew South America like the back of his hand and could move in any direction from a given point without the need of a map. True, they knew where the estate was located, but what if the unexpected happened? What if the plane went down? What if they moved the prisoners? No, there were too many ifs and maybes. He needed McGee.

Jake reached over and grabbed B.J.'s arm. He said, "Uh-oh, this could be bad!" Jake nodded toward Colonel Karpov, who was crossing the floor for the doors and Hatcher McGee.

McGee heard someone behind him. Turning, he gave the Russian colonel a look that would have scared the tail off the devil himself.

McGee's jaw set tight and the muscles in his face hardened as the man stepped up to him and said, "Commander McGee, I wish to apologize for not having known that you were made to endure the hardships of a prisoner of war during the Vietnam War. It was not a pleasant affair, I am sure. Nothing about that war was. It was a conflict in which my country should not have become involved."

McGee was taken aback momentarily by the man's statement. It seemed strange to hear that kind of talk from an officer of the army McGee had often called the Darth Vaders of the universe. To make matters worse, the bastard actually sounded sincere.

McGee's tone was threatening as he forced his jaw apart and snarled, "Colonel, I don't need nor do I want your fucking sympathy. And you can save that psychological Red Army bullshit of yours for those poor bastards in the Third World countries who have their necks firmly planted under your damn goose-steppin' jackboots."

The colonel's face was devoid of expression. His penetrating eyes seemed to be staring straight through McGee.

"I am sorry you feel that way, Commander. It is hardly an attitude that I feel secure with, considering the lives of my men may be at risk. A proper attitude is essential before any battle, Mr. McGee. As an officer, I am sure you are aware of that," said Karpov calmly. His eyes never wavered from those of the Navy SEAL.

The veins in McGee's neck were beginning to bulge and his face was reddening as he replied, "Maybe I need an attitude adjustment, Colonel. Perhaps you would like to attend to that little problem? Although I highly doubt you are capable of the job. Few men are—especially those who need four men to hold their victims while they work them over with a bamboo stick." McGee paused to watch Karpov's eyes flinch. His taunting was getting to the iron man. "What's the matter, Colonel? Little different when someone doesn't have his hands tied behind his back, isn't it? Why don't we just step outside and you can show me the error of my ways?"

All conversation in the hangar had stopped. Everyone stared at the two men at the door. Sound carried in the empty hangar. They had all heard the challenge issued by McGee. Karpov realized he had misjudged the resentment and bitterness harbored deep within this man. Yet, he could understand it. He had seen the same hatred in the eyes of the young men returning from the hell in Afghanistan. Now he had placed himself in a position where he must either fight this man or face the questioning looks of his own men. This had not been his purpose in coming to talk with McGee. His apology had been sincere. Now, what to do?

"Come on, Colonel," said McGee, waving toward the open area before the doors. "Let's just see what you've got."

Karpov assessed the man. They were both about the same size. It would be an interesting encounter, of that he had little doubt. McGee's tree-trunk arms and powerful, broad chest showed a man of endurance. His eyes were determined. "As you wish, Commander," said the colonel as he stepped past

McGee and walked out the doors. If Karpov held any fear of this man, it didn't show in his face.

McGee smiled widely as he turned to follow the man outside.

"Commander McGee!" shouted Mattson as he and the others walked to the doors. "That will be enough, Commander. You want a fucking fight, that's fine. Put your ass on that plane out there. I've got about a hundred motherfuckers armed to the teeth who are just waiting to give you all the fucking fight you want. But there won't be any fighting here, mister! You got that?"

McGee stood staring at Mattson. He didn't know B.J. as well as he did Jake. It was clear in Mattson's eyes that he meant what he said.

Karpov came back into the hangar.

McGee said, "Colonel, seems like there are a few folks here who don't want to see you get hurt. You ever feel up to dealing with my attitude, I want you to feel free to come to me any time."

Hatcher gave Mattson another look, then walked out of the hangar for the C-130 that had lowered its back ramp and was beginning to fire up its engines.

Karpov wasn't sure if he was glad B.J. had stopped the confrontation. They all realized it was only a matter of time before the two big men would have to square off against one another. B.J. knew that. But this wasn't the time nor the place.

"Let's get loaded up," said B.J. as he gave the colonel an understanding look.

Karpov turned and walked toward the plane. His men, separating from the Americans with whom they had been talking so freely before, now fell in silently beside their commander. There were still two teams boarding the plane, rather than the one united team Mattson and the general had hoped for. On board, the Spetsnaz team sat at the rear of the plane, the Americans forward toward the cockpit. The distance that separated them was infinitely more than nylon webbing and fifty feet of steel floor.

CHAPTER 8

2200 hours—June 22
Medina estate

Arias prepared two rum and Cokes and passed one to Medina, who sat at the end of the bar, deep in thought. Medina glanced up at the clock behind the bar for the third time. Ten o'clock. It had now been thirty hours since their demands had been delivered to the Russian embassy and there still was no reply. If this Colonel Molotov were the important man that Arias claimed, why had the Russians not immediately tried to negotiate for his release? The question lingered in Medina's mind as he slowly stirred his drink. Had he gone too far this time? After all, these were not Latin American officials or corrupt generals he was dealing with, but the two most powerful countries in the world, neither of which was going to appreciate the killing of two of their people and the kidnaping of the others. Yet, it was Molotov who had brought this down on his own head. He, Medina, had tried to deal in good faith with the Russian. He had upheld his portion of the agreement. It was Molotov who had taken his money and then tried to run. He had no choice but to stop the man. He could not be made to look like a fool before the other members of the cartel. Had it not been for the alertness of his drug connections in Europe and their timely call, Molotov would have succeeded in his escape to Russia. He felt Arias had not exercised good judgment in his methods of apprehending the Russians, but then, once gunshots were exchanged with the desperate men, it was reasonable to expect someone would be killed.

The Americans, however, were another matter. They should have been left out of this affair. He could have made a few calls to the right people and the matter would have been investigated as a another terrorist action against Americans in a Latin country. Now, it was too late for such a cover story. The Americans had seen the ranch, and Medina's name had been mentioned. The damage had already been done. The only thing to do now was to try to make the best of a bad situation. The money itself wasn't important. He would make more in a week than he had given Molotov for the entire operation. No, the money was not important, the ether was. The other cartel members were already suffering staggering losses for lack of the chemical. The two shipments that Molotov had delivered already gave him an edge on his competition. The final shipment he demanded for Molotov's release would assure him positive control of the largest drug cartel in the world. Dropping the swizzle stick next to the glass, he looked at the clock once more and sipped his drink. The reward was worth the risk.

Arias leaned forward on the bar. "They should have sent us a reply by now, Carlos. You know that, don't you?"

"Yes, I was just thinking the same thing," said Medina, setting his glass back on the bar.

"Perhaps they do not think we are serious about our threat. Maybe they need an example of just how serious we are about this."

Medina looked up at the man whom he had chosen as his chief lieutenant. He had treated him like a son, just as Petratina had done for him so many years ago. Arias did not have the patience nor the foresight to deal with unexpected problems reasonably as Medina had been forced to do when he was this man's age, but he was learning. Arias's answer to any problem was the gun. Medina could not fault the man for that, either. The willingness to use a weapon without question was what had brought Medina to this point and time in his life.

"What would you suggest we do, Rodrigo?" asked Medina.

Arias straightened and took a hefty drink from his glass before setting it down. A sinister grin formed at the corners of the man's lips and widened to the ends of his pencil-line mustache, as he said calmly, "We take the camcorder and the lights to the shed and film the prisoners. Then we execute one of the Americans. We point the weapon to the Russian colonel's head, and then let the picture fade out. I believe the Americans like to call such antics cliff-hangers. Then we can add the sound of a gun going off in the darkness, if you like. We will have the tape sent to both the Russian and American embassies. That should get us an immediate response from someone, don't you think?" asked Arias with a sadistic laugh.

Medina felt a sudden chill creep down his back. True, he had been a ruthless man in his day, but what Arias proposed convinced the drug lord that his lieutenant harbored an evil spirit unlike any he had ever known. Arias loved killing. Perhaps he loved it too much.

"You are serious, aren't you?" asked Medina softly.

"Of course. I guarantee you this will work, Carlos. And what is one more gringo, anyway? We did not ask them to come down here and interfere in our business. If they do, they should be prepared to pay the price."

Medina's powers of thought and decision making had not been as sharp since he had become addicted to the white powder. What Arias said made sense, but still a portion of his undamaged brain seemed to be trying to warn him against the idea. He took another drink and glanced at the clock again. Arias, seeing the indecision in the fat man's eyes, reached under the bar and removed a small bag of cocaine. Dumping the contents on the bar, he took a knife lying next to the limes and separated the pile into five even lines. Under Medina's watchful eye, Arias produced a slender silver tube from a pocket, leaned forward, placed a finger against one of his nostrils, and inhaled deeply as he moved his head forward and drew one of the lines up his nose. His eyes widened as he stood and snorted once, wiping the remnants of the powder from his nose.

"Come, Carlos, join me. If we must wait, we might as well feel good about it." Arias proffered the silver tube.

Medina stared at the powdered gold that lay before him. He momentarily fought back the urge, but the temptation was too overwhelming. Perhaps this would help him with his decision.

Arias smiled as he watched Medina inhale two of the lines, then pause before doing a third. Arias didn't care. He had no intention of using any more of the cocaine. He had only put five lines down because he knew once Medina began, he would not be able to stop. In a few minutes, he would have the permission he needed to execute one of the Americans.

Odie Watson checked to see that Captain Longly was asleep before he joined Sergeants Cochran and Foster in the corner of the small room. They spoke in whispers.

"I heard one of those guards complaining about their relief. They're planning on a changeover at midnight," said Watson as he held up his wrist to read the time. "It's a little past ten now. I figure by eleven, these guys will be gettin' pretty tired. They won't be thinking as quick as the guards coming on to relieve 'em. If we're gonna make a break, it's got to be while these guys are on."

"I think you're right, Top. How are we going to do it?" asked Foster, the youngest member of the group.

Watson was about to relate his plan when there came a commotion from outside. Peering through holes in the tin, the three Air Force men stared out to see what was going on. There was a quick exchange of Spanish between the guards, and a small group of men were walking toward the shed. What the hell, thought Watson. They weren't supposed to change over until midnight. What were those guys carrying? It sure as hell wasn't weapons.

"Quick, everybody, back over by the captain," said Watson. They took their positions just as the door swung open and Arias came in. Behind him, two men were carrying a set of lights on tripods. Another held a camera on his shoulder.

Captain Longly opened her eyes and sat up as Arias said, "Well now, are we all comfortable? I do so apologize for disturbing you, but I am afraid your government insists on having some type of proof that we are, in fact, holding you as prisoners. This should only take a moment."

Directing the men to set up the lights, Arias knelt down next to Molotov and pulled the old man up by his shoulders and leaned him against the wall. Molotov groaned loudly as his shattered leg was dragged across the floor of the shed. The leg was now twice its normal size and oozed a green putrid fluid from the bandages. The smell forced Arias to turn his head away and stand. Directing the cameraman to come forward, he pointed to Molotov. "Film this one first, but do not include the leg in the picture."

The lights were flipped on, and the man did as directed. Finished, he stepped back. Motioning for the Americans to move away from Molotov, he activated the camera again.

After thirty seconds, Arias stepped forward. "That should do it."

Now came the part he had been waiting for. The line of cocaine that he had inhaled to start Medina on his trip for the night had kicked in. Everything seemed funny now.

"Which one of you would like to address your ambassador? We plan to have this film delivered to your embassy by morning. Come now, which one of you would like to be a movie star for one night?" he said with a giggle.

Molotov opened his puffy red eyes and fought to comprehend what was happening. His power of mind over pain had evaporated hours ago. The agony of his leg teetered him on the verge of losing consciousness again. The young woman who had been caring for him stood and said, "I will be the spokesman for the group."

The man with the mustache quickly rejected the idea, insisting that one of the men step forward.

It was the haste with which the man had spoken that alerted Molotov to what he believed was about to happen. Lifting one arm slightly, he tried to speak. "No—no, he—is going to—"

Arias moved forward in one stride and kicked Molotov's wounded knee. The Russian screamed and instantly lost consciousness.

"You bastard!" shouted Longly as she knelt beside Molotov.

Arias realized that somehow the old man had figured out the

little game he had planned. He was not about to let the Russian interrupt his fun.

Smiling, Arias pointed to Watson, "How about you, Sergeant? Surely your ambassador could not resist a plea from a downtrodden, poor black man who has suffered years of oppression by the white man. Come, help your friends."

Watson spat at the man's feet. "Fuck you, you bean-eatin' asshole. I ain't beggin' nobody for nothin'."

Foster couldn't help himself. He laughed as he said, "You tell him, Top!"

"That one!" said Arias. Suddenly, two men stepped forward and pulled the young airman out into the center of the room.

"No. Leave him alone. I am the ranking person here. I should do this, not my men," cried Longly.

"I have other plans for you, bitch," said Arias as he directed the men to force Foster to his knees. "Now, pretty boy, I want you to put your hands together as if you are praying. Do it! Now!"

Foster's eyes were alive with fear and his heart was beating like a frightened puppy as he slowly followed Arias's command.

"Now, look into that camera and beg your ambassador to save you. It had better be convincing, boy, or we are going to let my men enjoy the night with your precious captain, here."

Foster was trembling. Try as he might, he couldn't stop. He had never known such fear in his life. But he had to do this for the captain. He couldn't let them hurt her. Slowly he began, "Mr. Ambassador, please, please help us—" Arias stepped to his side and slapped the boy hard behind the head, knocking him to the floor face first.

"You mumbling idiot. No one could understand that." Reaching forward, he grabbed Foster by the back of the shirt and pulled him back up to his knees. Stepping in front of him, he slapped the boy twice, hard, across the face.

Longly screamed for him to stop.

Watson and Cochran were cursing him. They were held at bay by a trio of gunmen.

Kneeling down, Arias placed his face only inches from

Foster's. "One more chance, boy. This time speak like you have a pair of balls. Do you hear me?"

Foster nodded that he understood, as Arias stood and moved to the side again. Blood was running down his chin from a busted lip. He placed his hands back together and looked up into the glass eye of the camera. Closing his eyes for a moment, he asked God to give him the strength to do this.

"Mr. Ambassador, please! Please help us. We—"

"No!" screamed Watson as he saw the pistol suddenly appear in the Colombian's hand and moved toward the back of Foster's head. The sound of the gun exploding in the small room drowned out Patrica Longly's cry.

Foster pitched forward to the floor. The cameraman cursed. Blood and brains from the chunk of skull that had been blown out of the right side of the boy's head had splattered onto the lens. Arias was laughing sadistically as he said, "Even special effects. What more could they want?"

Watson and Cochran, in shock at what they had just witnessed, slumped back against the wall and slid to the floor, unable to avert their eyes from the still twitching body. The twitching finally stopped, and both the men lowered their heads onto crossed arms that rested on their uplifted knees.

Pat Longly sat with her face against the wall and cried. She had lost another one. God, when would it stop?

Arias waved for the men to take the equipment outside. The combination of cocaine and the killing had put the man at the peak of his drug high. Now there remained only one other item to complete his night of fun. Bending down, he grabbed the captain by the shirt and pulled her up to her feet.

She screamed.

Watson and Cochran tried to stand, but were beaten back to the floor with vicious blows from the rifle butts of the trio that had been standing over them.

"Now, my little bitch, I shall take you to the house and demonstrate the sexual powers I derive from our number one selling product. It will take days before you walk normally again when I am finished with you. One young girl I satisfied for three days," laughed Arias.

Pat Longly struck out with all her might at the man,

slapping, scratching, kicking, doing all in her power to break away from Arias.

He only laughed at her. "I like women with spirit. The harder the fight, the better the fuck."

"You bastard. You laugh now, but you won't be laughing when they come for us. They're going to cut your throat from ear to ear," snapped Longly.

Arias stopped laughing and the grin disappeared from his face. What the hell was this bitch talking about? Slapping her once, he jerked her toward him. His foul breath almost overwhelmed her as he screamed, "Who? Who is coming? Who, bitch!"

For the first time, Longly saw a trace of fear in the man's eyes. "You are about as stupid as that ridiculous looking mustache. Did you really think you could just kill Americans and kidnap them without my country doing anything? You may have the leaders of this country scared of you and your drug lords, but we have something called the United States Special Operations Command, and they're not scared of anything, especially third-rate assholes like you," said Longly with a tone of satisfaction. She smiled and whispered, "And they're coming after you."

Arias slapped her again in an attempt to wipe the smirk from her face. "Your country may not enter this area. It would mean war with Brazil. There are rules of international law."

She was laughing now, exploiting the fear she had seen in those drug-crazed eyes. "That is why they are special, you uneducated bastard! They don't play by anyone's rules but their own. They're coming for you, all right—and they're going to kill you for what you've done here."

Arias pushed the woman away from him. She no longer had the frightened look of moments ago, nor he the sexual desire to attack her. Her words had brought Arias down from his floating high. Shouting for the men and the guards to get rid of Foster's body, he stormed out of the shed and headed for the house. He would have to ask Medina if what the woman said was true.

Reaching the door leading into the bar, Arias saw that Medina had passed the point of answering questions. He doubted if Medina could even tell him what planet they were on. Another bag of cocaine lay spread around the bar and on the floor. Medina sat, swaying back and forth, humming to himself, his eyes closed, and his face covered with the white powder.

Arias leaned against the doorway. What if the woman was right? These special soldiers, or whatever they were called, would be coming straight to Medina's estate. How many would there be? Fifty? A hundred? Maybe two hundred? There weren't enough men here. And besides, these cheap gunmen they had hired would be no match for professional soldiers. What should he do?

Arias stood silently pondering the problem. Then suddenly he smiled to himself as an idea began to form. "Of course, you use soldiers to fight soldiers. I will move the Russian and the Americans to our lab across the border in Brazil. The Amazon garrison there is the same as our own private army. They have well-equipped units that should be more than sufficient to discourage any planned attempt at coming after the prisoners."

Shouting out the front door for the leaders of the Medina drug soldiers, Arias gave orders to prepare the prisoners to be moved. They would be leaving for the border within the hour.

One of the men asked if Medina would be going.

Arias told him he would not.

This was going to work out better than he had hoped. If the woman was right and the American raiders did come, Medina was sure to be killed, leaving him, Arias, as the new drug lord of eastern Colombia. That pleasant thought made him forget his earlier fears. As a matter of fact, he now found himself inviting the arrival of the Americans. Now, if only the woman had not been exaggerating in the typical female fashion, he had no need to worry.

True to Patrica Longly's words, they were on their way.

CHAPTER 9

0100 hours—June 23
Base camp—Blue Boy
Colombia

The high-pitched whine of the hydraulics filled the aircraft as the rear ramp was lowered. Brian Ballock was the first man out of the aircraft. The others were instructed to wait until they had received the all clear from the CIA man before off-loading. Karpov was not surprised. This was a CIA installation. Four men dressed in camouflage fatigues gathered around Ballock. Karpov couldn't hear what they were saying, but it was apparent from the amount of arm waving and foot stomping going on, that the field operatives of this base were far from overjoyed at having a Russian Spetsnaz team deposited in their front yard.

B.J. and Jake moved to the rear of the aircraft where Karpov stood with his arm resting on one of the hydraulic lifts, watching the discussion going on a few feet to the rear of the plane.

"Colonel, we'll be off-loading in a few minutes. Mr. Ballock needs to clear up a few things first," said Mattson as he watched one of the men throw his jungle hat in the dirt and jab his finger at Ballock's face.

"That's quite all right, Major. I understand. I would no

doubt have a similar attitude were Mr. Yelintikov to arrive at my Spetsnaz school with a group of American commandos. However, I doubt if they have anything here at this base that we have not seen before."

Jake seemed surprised by Karpov's statement and asked, "What do you mean, Colonel?"

"Satellites, Commander," said Karpov. "I am certain that somewhere in our files in Moscow the GRU has enough information on this base to tell you the date and time the first bombs were dropped in this jungle to begin the construction, when it was completed, and how many personnel are here on a regular basis. They could even tell you the types of weapons and communications equipment presently in use—all from photographs," said the colonel with a grin.

Jake was stunned. "Your people got a fix on this base with a satellite?" he asked as B.J. began to smile with the Russian colonel.

"Yes, Commander. This one, as well as the other thirty-three similar to this one that your Central Intelligence Agency has established around the world."

"Damn. Is there anything you guys don't know about this place?" asked Jake.

Karpov thought for a moment, then replied. "Yes, as a matter of fact, there was something. The code name—Blue Boy."

Jake shook his head. "Shit—and now we gave that to you. Well, what the hell. If you've got all that other information, what's in a name!"

Karpov's grin dropped from his face. His penetrating eyes became serious. "Success is measured by precise and accurate intelligence information, Commander. There are no unimportant details—even in a name," said Karpov in his best classroom tone.

Jake knew when he was being chastised. God knows, he'd heard that tone of voice from more than a few of his professors at Harvard.

"Okay, lesson's over, Jake," said B.J. looking out at Ballock, who was waving for them to exit the aircraft. "Let's get the boys off this bird."

Jake nodded. "You got it, boss."

As he turned to leave, Karpov overheard the Navy man saying, "Thirty-three others—I'll be damned."

"He is a bright young man, Major," said the colonel. "He asked questions. That is good. My Major Suslov could learn from such a man."

"Yeah. Jake's not bad for a Harvard man, I guess. Shall we go, Colonel?" asked B.J. "I'd like to contact General Johnson and Mr. Yelintikov for an update on the situation."

"Of course, Major, after you."

Ballock led the two men to the communications center. Entering the room, Karpov could feel suspicious eyes on him which restored his faith in his belief that all intelligence personnel were naturally paranoid.

A short man in his early fifties with a receding hairline walked up to them. His name was Abe Hoskins, and he was Blue Boy's station chief. His voice was gruff. "Hell, why don't I just take my boys and go to the city for the weekend and let the Russians run this fuckin' place? What are you doing, bringing these people in here?"

Ballock placed his hands on his hips and squinted at Hoskins as he replied, "Oh, get off that shit, Abe. These boys are here by order of the president of the United States, and if that ain't good enough for you, then fuck off, or I'll turn 'em loose on these candy-ass, James Bonds. We need to contact the embassy in Bogotá. Either help us out or get out of the way."

Hoskins's face reddened, more from embarrassment than anger.

He and Ballock had worked together with the agency for over fifteen years. It was Hoskins who had pulled Ballock's head out the barrel of kerosene.

B.J. was afraid they were going to have problems with the man, but that idea disappeared as Hoskins reached out his hand to Karpov, smiled, and said, "Goofy son of a bitch has a mouth on him, don't he, Colonel? Name's Abe Hoskins. Pleasure to meet both of you gentlemen."

Karpov felt his firm grip and noted the genuine friendliness in the man's blue eyes. It made him feel good.

B.J. was relieved as well.

"Turner, get the embassy on the line," said Hoskins, speaking to a young radio operator in the corner.

"I take it some of your boys are not too happy about this arrangement, Abe," said Ballock as the group walked over to the radios.

"Awh, you know how kids are these days, Brian—seen too many of those damn Rambo movies, I guess. Oh, yeah, plane brought in all the equipment you guys ordered. Got it stored in the shed next to the longhouse. We can check it out after your call, if you want."

Both commanders agreed. The operator made the patch and handed the mike to B.J. "General Johnson's on the line, sir."

"Thank you. Sir, B.J. here. Just wanted to let you know we're on station and to get an update."

Mattson and Karpov detected a hint of concern in the general's voice as his words came over the speaker above the radio. "I was just getting ready to call you, B.J. The situation's changed since you left Panama. We have a report who the prisoners have been moved. We're still trying to get confirmation from a second source, but I'm afraid the information is going to prove correct."

"Did we get a new location or general area of the move, sir?" asked Mattson.

"Roger. Get your map and stand by. Out."

Hoskins and Ballock moved to the large map on the wall next to the radios, ready to plot the new location. Karpov joined them. The radio came to life again.

"B.J., we've narrowed it down to an area ten miles west of the town of São Gabriel along the Negro River inside Brazil. Medina's primary lab for processing cocaine is along that river somewhere. Our source says that is where they were moving them."

B.J. watched Hoskins mark the area as he said, "Sir, that's in Brazil. Is that going to cause us any diplomatic problems?"

"Mr. Yelintikov and I feel that we can handle that through our embassies in Brasilia. Our main concern is the reports that Medina has managed to buy off the Brazilian army detachment in that area. It's the Amazon Battalion, B.J.—a tough bunch of jungle fighters. If those reports are correct, you could be facing a larger force than we anticipated. We have agreed that if you and Colonel Karpov feel that the mission should be aborted due to this situation, we will stand by your decision. The choice is yours."

Mattson and Karpov stood looking at each other. All eyes in the room were on the two commanders. With Smith remaining at the base with the choppers, they would only have thirteen men on the ground. Was that enough? Taking on the ragtag army of a drug dealer was one thing, but taking on a well-trained jungle battalion was another story. The Medina estate had been a fixed location, complete with photos. The new location was somewhere along the Negro River in country familiar to the Amazon Battalion, and to only one member of the team, Hatcher McGee, the only man in the group who was not doing well with the team-player theory. His attitude could have disastrous results for everyone, McGee included. The general was still waiting for a reply.

Karpov moved away from the map and stepped to B.J.'s side.

"We have come this far, Major. Our goal lies less than 150 miles to the east. As for me and my men, I see no reason to let our comrades linger in this man's grasp any longer. I believe we should continue, no matter what the odds," said Karpov with a determined look on his face.

Mattson stared at the map once more. What the hell, this was what they were paid to do. "I agree, Colonel."

Keying the mike, he relayed that message to the general, who paused, then replied in a tone that clearly held a sense of pride in the decision that had been made.

"Very well, Major. I know that if it can be accomplished with any degree of success at all, we have the men there who can do it. We will keep you informed of any more changes should they occur before takeoff. Are we still looking at a three-hour window for the drop?" asked Johnson.

Mattson looked to Karpov who nodded in the affirmative.

"Roger, sir. Estimated time in target area approximately 0430 hours. We will contact Blue Boy via satellite once we have regrouped on the ground."

Johnson wished them luck and signed off.

The men in the room were still staring at the two team leaders, trying to comprehend how thirteen men thought they could fight their way through an army and rescue anybody.

"Mr. Hoskins, we'd like to get our equipment now, if you don't mind," said B.J.

"Certainly, Major. If you and the colonel will follow me—" Turning to Ballock, the station chief said, "Brian, you had better get the C-130 pilots in here and show them the new target area. They'll have to modify their flight plan and pick out some new reference points to use as a guide going in."

Ballock agreed. Once outside, he broke off from the group and headed for the plane while the others walked across the camp toward two heavy-duty conex containers secured with large Evergreen locks. Seeing Jake in the doorway of the longhouse, B.J. yelled for him to bring the team to help move the equipment inside. Within the hour, each man was assembling his web gear, rigging rucksacks, and securing the hundred-foot ropes that were going to be needed to rappel from the trees to the jungle floor. Weapons were test-fired, then disassembled, cleaned, and oiled. Feelings of tension and anticipation slowly wore away the barriers that might have existed between the men when they left Panama. Mitchell and Fletcher helped some of the Russians rig their rucksacks. Adams and Jake worked with Suslov and Trotsky in the breakdown of the ammunition and grenades, while Karpov and B.J. made a more detailed study of the suspected area of the drug lab. Everyone was doing something to help someone else; everyone but McGee, who sat in a corner of the room, reassembling the sawed-off automatic twelve gauge shotgun he had requested. Sergeant Issak Gorki, seeing the weapon in McGee's hands, finished his rigging and walked over to McGee.

"Comrade Commander," said the young Russian, "could I possibly see that weapon for a moment?"

McGee snapped the last pin into place, worked the slide three times in rapid succession, then looked up at Gorki. "Get the fuck away from me, kid, before I load this thing and give you an up close and personal view of the business end of this baby."

Karpov heard the remark and saw the dejected look on his sergeant's face. Snapping the pencil he held in his hand, he tossed it to the floor.

B.J. saw the fire in the big man's eyes as he turned away from the map and started across the room.

McGee saw him coming and tossed the shotgun on the bed. "Uh-oh, looks like the colonel thinks it time for that attitude adjustment," he said tauntingly, rolling his long fingers into two barrel-like fists. "Well, come on, Colonel. Like I said, any time you feel lucky."

Jake stepped in front of McGee while B.J. hurried in front of Karpov. "Colonel, this won't serve any worthwhile purpose, and you know it."

Karpov was about to push Mattson out of the way, when Ballock walked into the room. The agency man paused, quickly assessing the situation. He almost wished he had come in a few minutes later.

"Colonel Karpov—Major! The general's on the line again. Wants to talk to you right away. Colonel, Mr. Yelintikov has something for you, too."

The tension in the room was thick enough to be cut with a knife as McGee and Karpov stared across the short span of thirty feet at each other.

B.J., his hand still on the man's arm, nodded toward the door. "Come on, Colonel. They're waiting."

Karpov pivoted on his heel and stomped out of the room, almost tearing the screen door off the building as he flung it open. Mattson shot a look of disapproval at McGee, who only grinned, retrieved the shotgun, and sat back down on the bed.

Johnson sounded tired. The sadness in his voice indicated more bad news. The analysis was correct. Johnson went on to explain that the Russian and American embassies had just received Arias's videotape of Sergeant Foster's execution. He included a description of the prisoner's condition and a vivid account of the killing of the young airman. The detailed description of the murder visibly bothered those in the room who had gathered around the radio. The execution had been carried out as a warning of what would happen to the others if the demands were not met. Mattson's teeth meshed and the muscles in his jaw tensed as the general finished.

"Sorry, B.J. Seems like all I've been doing is passing on bad news. But I knew you'd have to know about this. That means there's only Molotov and three Americans in that camp."

Between this new development and McGee's constant taunting of Colonel Karpov, B.J. was beginning to feel that Murphy's Law was working overtime on this operation.

"Not your fault, sir," said B.J. "We'll be taking off within the hour. I don't want to waste any more time. Sooner we're in there, the sooner we start collecting payback for this bullshit."

"Major, I'm afraid there's one more thing. Is Colonel Karpov with you?"

Mattson sighed. Jesus, what else could be wrong? "Yes, sir. He's standing right next to me."

"Fine. Put him on the radio. Mr. Yelintikov has some news for him. You might want to hear this, too, B.J. Here he is."

Yelintikov's tone sounded no more positive than General Johnson's had as he said, "Colonel, do you know a Lieutenant Mikal?"

Karpov stiffened. "Ye—yes, sir. One of my best officers and an exceptional student when he was in the course. Why, sir?"

"Lieutenant Mikal was arrested by the KGB three hours ago at the Moscow airport. He had tickets and false passports for Brazil. Under extensive questioning—" Yelintikov paused and and carefully recanted his statement. "When questioned, Mikal admitted his part in this affair and also provided us with the names of the other officers involved."

Karpov bit his lower lip as he stared at the mike in his hand. Yelintikov had been right the first time. Extensive questioning was the only way the KGB could have gotten that information from the young lieutenant. The thought of the KGB employing their ruthless tactics of interrogation on one of his Spetsnaz officers made him sick to his stomach. Mattson could see the pain in the colonel's eyes as Yelintikov paused a moment then said, "Colonel, Mikal has informed us that Yuri Molotov, the colonel's son, is dead."

Karpov's fist tightened around the mike. All of Nikolai

Molotov's efforts—this entire business—had been for nothing. If rescued, the hero would face trial and disgrace. Young Russian officers with promising careers were being arrested. Americans had been drawn, by accident, into this scheme. Two had already died, and there was a good chance more would die before this was over. And all for what? A father's desperate attempt to do what his country would not do: save his son. A son who was now dead. Karpov was trying to regain his composure, but was having a difficult time of it. "Comrade Yelintikov, I—would appreciate it if you would see that Lieutenant Mikal is released from KGB headquarters and placed in a military confinement facility until my return. I would like to testify in his defense."

"Colonel, I—I'm afraid that's not possible. Lieutenant—"

Karpov interrupted. "Sir, please. I am certain we can prove there were circumstances that—"

"Colonel Karpov," said Yelintikov, his voice shaking, "Lieutenant Mikal is dead. He hung himself in his cell less than an hour ago."

The words sent a solemn silence over the room. B.J. watched the big colonel lean forward against the radios and close his eyes.

Passing the mike back to Mattson, Karpov turned and left the room. "Colonel—Colonel, are you still there?" asked Yelintikov. B.J. informed the man that the colonel had left the room. Yelintikov replied that he understood. Before signing off, he asked that B.J. pass the colonel a message. "Tell Colonel Karpov that, just as the star of the czar shines in the vault of the Kremlin, so shall the life of Molotov."

Mattson promised to pass on the message and signed off. Outside, Karpov stared up at the sky. B.J. detected a glimmer of moonlight reflecting off the tears in the big man's eyes.

"Colonel Karpov, I'm sorry about Colonel Molotov's son and your lieutenant," said Mattson softly.

"Thank you, Major. That is very kind of you. You know, I often wonder what makes a man want to be a soldier. The hours are long and the pay next to nothing. You endure physical hardships to strengthen the body and mind, only to have them both blown apart in some far corner of the world for people who could care less for the suffering of the soldier. I—I—Lieutenant Mikal was a good soldier, Major," said Karpov, his voice trailing off as he leaned his head against the wall. He was silent.

Mattson knew the pain the man was feeling. He had been there before, himself. It was a pain that was endured by every soldier, in every army, worldwide, who had ever lost a friend. That loss forever marks the warrior's heart.

Leaving Karpov with his thoughts, B.J. walked quietly away and returned to the longhouse. The colonel would join them when he was ready.

Jake was standing outside when B.J. arrived. Mattson told him what had happened.

"How's the colonel holding up?" Jake asked.

"He'll be fine, Jake. He's just looking for a few answers to some hard questions," replied Mattson. "How are we coming in here? About ready to tell the pilots to fire up the engines?"

Jake told him they were ready to go, but that things were still a little tense between McGee and the Russian communicator, Gorki.

No sooner had Jake said that than the sounds of a scuffle broke out. Shouting and yelling erupted from inside the longhouse. B.J. and Jake reached the door just as Sergeant Issak Gorki came flying headfirst through the screen door and hit the ground hard. The Russian's face was a bloody mess. McGee came out next, tearing the screen door off its hinges as he yelled, "Told you to stay away from me, you little Russian fuck!"

Gorki was struggling to get up, but could only manage to rise to his hands and knees.

McGee circled around the battered man. "Come on! Come on, you asshole—get up!"

B.J. was about to move in on McGee when Jake grabbed his arm, shook his head, then nodded, past McGee.

Colonel Alexei Karpov stopped two steps behind the big Navy SEAL and yelled, "Commander McGee!"

McGee turned to face the Russian.

Karpov's huge fist came around like a freight train, catching McGee square in the mouth and sending the big man six feet back and to the ground. Reaching down with one hand, the colonel lifted Gorki straight up onto his feet and gently nudged him off to the side. Closing the distance to McGee, he looked down and said, "It's time—Mr. McGee!"

McGee smiled broadly, forcing more blood from his split lips. He spat and climbed to his feet.

The team members looked to Mattson to see if he intended to stop the fight.

Jake whispered, "Might as well let 'em get it over with."

"I agree," said B.J. "Okay—everybody get back and give 'em room. We're going to settle this shit once and for all."

Seeing Ballock and the others from the commo shed running up, B.J. yelled, "Ballock, keep those people back. Nobody interferes."

McGee rubbed his hands on his pants as he continued to smile.

The two men circled. Their fists were raised and their eyes took in every movement of the other.

"You're gonna be going home without any teeth, Colonel," said McGee.

"I am not the one with blood on his face, Commander," replied Karpov. "On that ugly face of yours, missing teeth would be an improvement."

McGee yelled, "Motherfucker—say your prayers!" as he stepped in with a powerful, two-fisted combination. Karpov blocked his right, but McGee's left came screaming through, catching him above the right eye and sending him staggering backward on unsteady feet. McGee kept coming, another right, then a left that missed. That left an opening for Karpov, who brought an overhand right straight down. The crunching blow glanced off McGee's temple, but still hit with enough force to daze the big man who stepped backward and shook his head to clear his momentarily blurred vision. Karpov moved in on his prey, but he had waited too long. McGee ducked the Russian's right-handed windmill swing and brought his fist straight up into the man's gut with a force that brought the colonel's feet six inches off the ground. Air shot out of Karpov's body in an instant. His face reddened quickly as he gasped to get air back into his burning lungs. McGee, knowing the man was in trouble, delivered a shot to the colonel's head and sent him tumbling to the ground.

The crowd around them was going wild. The Russians were yelling for their commander to get up. The Americans, except for Mattson, were screaming for McGee to move in for the kill.

B.J. noticed that Mitchell wasn't cheering much, either. Hatcher was Mitch's friend and a fellow SEAL, but Hatch's whole attitude from the very beginning had cast a shadow over this mission. He had hoped the general's talk about forgetting the past would help, but it hadn't. Colonel Karpov hadn't been the man responsible for McGee's years as a POW. However, this chance to wreak vengeance upon this man he saw as a symbol could ease his years of bitterness and pain and just maybe serve some worthwhile purpose in the end.

Jake tried to refrain from showing emotion either way, but no one could change years of being taught that the Russians were the bad guys, and the Americans were the heroes of the world, riding to the rescue. It was the same with the other Americans watching these two giants slugging it out.

McGee stepped back and allowed Karpov to get to his feet, then beckoned for the colonel to come on back for more. Karpov didn't disappoint him. McGee blocked both blows as the Russian came in swinging. He delivered an elbow to the bridge of the colonel's nose, which emitted a sickening, crunching sound. The sound brought a low murmur of moans from the circle of observers. Karpov's nose was broken. Blood streamed down the front of his shirt as he staggered back. McGee came at him full force. Both men tumbled to the ground. Locked together in a viselike grip, they rolled back and forth, raining blow after blow into each other's face and body, until finally, neither man could lift his aching, weary arms.

Ballock circled the group and stepped up next to B.J. saying, "Major, you better put an end to this or they're going to kill each other."

Mattson didn't answer. This was something that was going to run its course. Both men were now on their knees, bloody and battered. Their faces were swollen and red. They alternated blows to each other's face, each determined that he would not be the one to quit. The cheering had stopped now, replaced by the realization that they were watching a battle between two men who possessed wills so strong that they would rather die than yield. Twenty minutes had passed since the fight began. Both men now sat on the backs of bent legs, less than three feet apart, staring at each other. Neither was able to lift his arms. It was over.

"Mitch, you and Fletcher get McGee inside and clean him up. Then I want to talk to him. Jake, you see to it that the rest of the people get their gear on board and stand by. We're out of here in the next thirty minutes. Let's move it!" barked B.J.

The Russians helped their battered commander to his feet. They led him away to the camp dispensary.

Ballock stood shaking his head as he said, "Damnedest fight I've ever seen—and I've seen some good ones, let me tell you. What are you going to do now, Major?"

It was clear by Mattson's face that the man was disgusted with the whole business, and he took it out on Ballock. "My fucking job, Mr. Ballock—that's what you fucking people want, isn't it? Or would you prefer I schedule another goddamn fight for your fucking benefit!"

Ballock didn't dare say another word. The major was working on a short fuse, and he wasn't about to be the one caught in the blast when B.J. went off. Raising his hands, he simply nodded and walked away. He already had enough scars under his eyes.

Jake came back outside. "B.J., McGee wants to talk to you. I told him about the videotape and the KGB business. I think he's kind of regretting all this now."

Mattson's temper still hadn't cooled. "Well ain't that just fuckin' sweet of the son of a bitch. He hasn't done anything but fuck this thing up from the beginning. Well, I'm sorry the guy was a fucking prisoner of war. I'm sorry he has a fuckin' problem dealing with the past, but goddamn it, Jake, life goes on! McGee wants to hold onto his fuckin' nightmares all his life, then fine. I don't need the bastard that bad. I'd rather wander around out there lost than put up with any more of his shit! He's out! Snake Adams has worked the area before. We'll put Mitch and Sergeant Zhukov on the point. McGee stays with Smith and the choppers. That's a motherfuckin' order!"

Jake Mortimer started to say something in McGee's defense, but like Ballock, Mortimer saw the fire in B.J.'s eyes and realized this wasn't the time. "I'll tell him."

"You do that. Then get your butt on that plane. We've wasted enough goddamn time with this kiddy shit," said B.J. as he turned and walked off toward the dispensary.

Mortimer took a deep breath as he watched his partner and friend walk away. This was his fourth mission with B.J. and he had never before seen the man this upset. The decision to leave McGee behind had not been an easy one. Jake knew that, and he was right. They were acting like a bunch of school kids watching a street fight while some hopped-up dude was blowing Americans away and filming it for the fun of it. Captain Pat could be next. The entire situation was no more than one huge stress factor, and B.J. was trying to hold it all together by himself. Jake didn't envy him that job.

After he went back inside, Tommy Smith came over and told Jake the choppers were ready. He wanted to know what all the yelling had been about.

Jake told him not to ask, then went inside to tell McGee the news, advising the Navy man to leave it alone unless he was prepared to go at it again with B.J. Mattson.

McGee wasn't. He couldn't see out of one eye, and he was having a hard time breathing because of three broken ribs in his right side. Hatcher McGee didn't feel that he had lost the fight, but then, he wasn't exactly feeling like a winner, either.

CHAPTER 10

Thirty minutes out, the crew chief of the C-130 switched on the red lights to soften the strain on the men's eyes. This would allow for quick adjustment of their night vision once they were out of the aircraft and free-falling to the jungle below. The haunting, dull glow of the crimson color bathed the interior of the airplane, giving it and the team a supernatural appearance. B.J. and Colonel Karpov sat on the right with half of the team. Jake and Major Suslov were on the left with the other half. The heavy droning of the engines hummed with a steady rhythm, lulling some of the men to sleep while others stared at nothing in particular and thought their private thoughts. No one spoke. There were occasional glances and nervous smiles exchanged as eyes roamed the interior of the plane and came to rest on a teammate across the aisle. No matter how many airborne operations a paratrooper made, there was always that nervous twinge in the pit of his stomach from the adrenaline flow. That twinge was barely noticeable at first, but always there, building with each beat of the heart and increasing as each minute brought them closer to their target.

B.J. glanced out of the corner of his eye at Karpov and the Band-Aid Doc had placed across the colonel's broken nose after he had set it. One eye was puffy and discolored; shades of black were already spreading outward under his eyes. The other was swollen above the eyebrow. Doc had told the colonel that he might have sustained one or more broken ribs in the fight, but Karpov had insisted they were only bruised and that he was fine. B.J. didn't buy that. He had noticed the pain in the colonel's face as they had chuted up and the weight of the rucksacks was added to the parachute harness. There was little doubt that Colonel Karpov was a hard man with an iron constitution and the inner strength to ignore pain. Russian or no Russian, Mattson had nothing but respect for the man.

Lieutenant Chivenov, the medical officer, had taken B.J. off to the side and suggested that, if possible, they should lower their planned jump altitude of twelve thousand feet to nine thousand. With a broken nose and probable rib damage, the colonel was going to have a hard time breathing as it was. Mattson agreed and informed the team of the change during the jumpmaster checks that had been made on board the plane.

Surprisingly enough, the only person in the unit to object to B.J.'s decision to leave McGee behind was Colonel Karpov, who argued that for all of his faults, the big man was the only one who truly knew the target area. He had asked B.J. to reconsider his decision. Mattson had refused. McGee would work with Smith and the chopper crews, handling one of the door-mounted mini-guns if close air support should be required.

The crew chief placed his hand to the headset he was wearing, then waved for B.J. to come to the rear of the airplane.

Struggling out of his seat with the sixty-pound rucksack bouncing against his knees, Mattson waddled back to the chief, who cupped his hands to yell above the engine noise. "Pilot says we're twenty minutes out, Major."

Mattson nodded and turned to the team, holding up both hands. He opened and closed them twice, signifying the twenty-minute warning.

Jake pointed to Adams and motioned for the man to wake up Mitchell and Fletcher, who were sleeping next to him.

The adrenaline began to flow a little faster now as all heads turned to the rear of the aircraft. All eyes were on Mattson. Palms began to sweat as seconds turned slowly into minutes that seemed like hours. Nervous hands checked and rechecked a piece of equipment here, a piece there, and back to the first one again. Anything to take one's mind off the clock and the ever increasing noise of the engines that seemed to grow louder and louder as they came closer to their target.

The chief tapped B.J. on the arm again. "Ten minutes."

Mattson gave the signal and adjusted the position of the MP5 9mm submachine gun attached to his right leg. His fingers then went up to the small black button attached to his collar. No larger than a quarter, the disklike object was a micro-receiver. Each man was wearing one. The receivers were provided by the CIA. B.J. had elected to have the colonel carry the transponder homing device which was no larger than a cigarette pack. When activated, it would emit a silent signal. Once they had made their crash landings into the treetops, each man in the team would use his rope to rappel to the ground. Once he had secured his weapon and rucksack, he would activate the button and turn until the disk began to emit a soft beeping sound. By following this signal, they would all move toward Colonel Karpov's position. If the signal began to fade, they would only have to stop and turn slowly until the signal became strong again. Then they would move in that direction. Once everyone was accounted for, they would move out to the Negro River and begin the search for the lab.

"Five minutes, Major!" yelled the chief as he reached up and punched a black button on the side of the aircraft. There was a loud click, followed by the whine of hydraulics and a sudden gush of cool air as the seal along the rear ramp broke and the huge door began to lower itself like an old-fashioned drawbridge over the moat of darkness below. Mattson pointed at Jake and Karpov, then he raised his hands, signaling for the two men to get the team on their feet.

The men on both sides stood up. In an effort to steady themselves as wind turbulence caused the aircraft to rock and dip like an unsteady roller coaster, they grasped the nylon netting of the seats along the walls of the plane.

Mattson waved for the men to move forward.

Shuffling their feet, they inched their way toward the rear of the aircraft and the gaping black hole that appeared as the ramp locked into place. The wind whipped through the plane, pulling at pants legs and shirtsleeves. The noise was deafening. Mattson brought the men to the very edge of the ramp and looked at the chief, who held up two fingers. Karpov and Jake acknowledged that they had seen the two-minute warning.

Hearts pounded as the adrenaline flowed full force; B.J. turned his back to the others and first stared down into the sea of blackness below, then to the indicator lights at the corner of the ramp.

The red lamp went out and the green light came on. Mattson didn't hesitate. Bending his knees slightly, he leaped forward into the nothingness of the night air and began to fall, the others following him out. Within five seconds, the only man left near the ramp was the crew chief.

The rushing air fluttered Mattson's clothes as his speed accelerated and he fell faster toward the blackness below. Turning his head slightly, he looked back up and over his shoulder. He could see the others silhouetted like shadowy birds in the moonlight. Below, a silver streak, glittering with moonbeams, darted in and out of the blackness. This was the Negro River.

B.J.'s altimeter signaled that he was at 3,500 feet. Gripping the rip cord handle, he pulled it. The chute fluttered as it unfolded from the backpack. There was a sudden jerk as the chute filled with air. B.J. reached up for the toggles along the risers and began to steer himself toward the trees bordering the river. The only sound he could hear were the other parachutes opening somewhere above him.

Studying the terrain below, he tried to decide where he wanted to land. Then he whispered, "Hell with it! A tree's a tree." Guiding in on the giants below, he prepared himself for the impact. It wasn't going to be a pleasant experience.

His boots crashed through first, followed by his body and his equipment. Limbs snapped and whipped his face and hands as he continued to fall through the top of the seventy-five-foot tree. He stopped suddenly and was flung back hard against a large limb, sending a sharp pain down his back and into his legs. B.J. could hear the snapping and cracking of tree limbs as the others crashed into the trees around him. Relaxing a moment to allow the adrenaline flow to return to normal, B.J.

breathed deeply of the moist, loam-scented air, the warm breath of an old friend—the jungle.

Unhooking his harness and securing the rucksack to his rappelling rope, he adjusted the snap-links in his Swiss seat and began to work his way toward the ground.

Midway down, he paused. His heart jumped as he saw a pair of yellow eyes with black, diamond-shaped pupils staring out of the leaves at him. He had no idea what it was nor did he care to find out.

Kicking out, he slid the rest of the way to the ground. His boots came to rest on the moist, spongy surface of the jungle floor. The aroma of rotten vegetation mixed with warm air rose up to greet him. Untying the rucksack, he swung it up on his shoulders as he checked his weapon. Activating the disk, B.J. began a slow, 360-degree turn, until the small device began to beep. Karpov was due north of his position. Quietly, and with the experience born of jungle war, Mattson picked his way through the thick brush and vines as he moved to the linkup point.

Colonel Karpov leaned back against the broad-based tree and took shallow breaths. His side was killing him. The rough landing, combined with the rappelling, had taken their toll on the man of iron. The transponder, its faint red light indicating that it was on, hung from a branch next to him. No one had arrived yet. Occasionally, he would pick up the sounds of the men who were working their way toward him. Wiping the sweat from his brow, he flinched as his hand touched the swollen area above his left eye. McGee must have a right hand made of steel, thought Karpov as he pulled his hand away. It was too bad that Mattson hadn't reconsidered bringing the man along. Anyone who could fight that well with his hands must be hell on wheels in a firefight.

Karpov heard a twig snap near him. Shifting his AK-47 in the direction, he eased the safety off. It should be one of the team, but he didn't want any surprises.

Mattson emerged from the palms but stopped as he stared down the barrel of the Russian weapon. Karpov flipped the safety back on and leaned the rifle against the tree. B.J. pulled the pack from his back, dropping it to the ground. He sat down beside the colonel.

"Anybody else in yet?" he asked.

"No, you are the first, Major."

"How's the ribs?" asked B.J. noting the short breaths the Russian was taking.

"I am fine, Major. It will be daylight soon. Do you still plan to move at first light?"

"Yes. We'll have to split up into two teams. We don't know if that lab is located upriver or downriver. I'll take your tracker, Sergeant Zhukov, with me. You can take Mitchell. First one who finds anything calls in the location, and we regroup. Once we find the lab, we'll have to play it by ear. Not exactly as well planned as the Normandy Invasion, but it'll do. What do you think, Colonel?"

Karpov managed a smile as he said, "I believe that, given our situation, it is the most logical plan, Major."

The first traces of gray were beginning to spread along the horizon as the final members of the team broke through the brush and knelt around Mattson. High in the treetops, the howler monkeys began their early-morning concert of high-pitched screams. Flocks of birds ruffled their feathers and greeted the morning with strange calls like no others on earth: rusty gates, shrill traffic whistles, foghorns, animal howls, beeps, clicks, and roars, but the strangest sound of all was the persistent clanging of a bell. This last was the mysterious bellbird. Jack Adams told them few men had ever seen this strange bird. Its clear, haunting tones had led many an unsuspecting soul, who, lost, followed the sound to their death in the depths of the wilderness, believing they were nearing civilization. It was morning. The jungle of Brazil was coming alive to greet the sun and the uninvited guests who had fallen from the sky.

B.J. made a second count to make sure they had everyone. He asked if there were any injuries. There were none. That was a good sign; at least they had begun with lady luck on their side. Mattson detailed the plan, then divided the team into two groups of six men each. Colonel Karpov would lead one group with Jake, Mitchell, Lieutenant Chivenov, Kerenski, and Gorki. B.J. would lead Major Suslov, Adams, Fletcher, Zhukov, and Sergeant Trotsky. The river lay fifty yards to their north. B.J. would work his way upriver while Karpov would move in the opposite direction. He reminded the men of the fact that the Brazilian army units in this area were on the payroll of the drug cartel. Therefore, there were no friendlies in this area of operation. They hoped to move without detection, but if they should encounter an army patrol, they would have to kill them all. One survivor could sound the alarm and the whole Amazon Battalion would be down on them before the sun set.

Karpov sent Mitchell out on the point and his men followed the big Navy SEAL off into the jungle. The colonel shook hands with B.J. "Good hunting, my friend. Let's hope we can pick up the trail quickly."

Mattson pumped the man's hand warmly and replied, "The same to you, Colonel. With a little luck, this time tomorrow we'll be on board one of those Blue Boy helicopters with our people and heading home."

Karpov smiled and nodded approvingly. He turned to follow the others.

Mattson suddenly remembered he hadn't given the colonel Yelintikov's message.

"Oh, yeah, Colonel," he said, "Mr. Yelintikov wanted me to tell you that as long as the star of the czar shines in the Kremlin vault so will the life of Colonel Molotov."

Colonel Karpov stopped dead in his tracks with his back to Mattson. He asked, "Are you certain he said the star of the czar, Major?"

B.J. thought about it for a moment, then replied, "Yes, Colonel, I'm positive. Why? Is there something I should know?"

Karpov stood silent for a few seconds. The fingers of his right hand clutched the pistol grip of the AK-47 so tightly that B.J. could see the knuckles of his hand turning white.

Something was wrong. B.J. wasn't sure what it was, but he had heard it in the man's voice. The feeling was reaffirmed by the grip the Russian held on the weapon. "Colonel, what is it?" asked Mattson.

Karpov, his back still to B.J., answered, "It is nothing, Major—only an old phrase I have not heard in many years. I will see you later, Major. Good luck." Then the colonel disappeared into the jungle.

Adams came up to Mattson. "We're ready to move out, B.J."

"Yeah—okay, Jack. I want you and Zhukov on the point, then Trotsky, Suslov, and Fletcher. I'll bring up the rear."

"You got it," said Jake, who paused a moment, then asked, "Is there anything wrong, B.J.?"

Mattson was running the phrase over and over in his mind. It meant nothing to him, but it had certainly meant something to Karpov. The man had stepped off into the jungle as if he were bearing the burdens of the world on his shoulders. B.J. turned around and looked at Jack. He said, "I can't answer that question, Jack, more like a sixth sense thing, I guess." Mattson saw the confusion in Adams's eyes. "Oh, hell—maybe I'm just getting old and paranoid. Come on—let's go."

By 8:00 A.M. the heat and humidity of the triple canopy had turned the jungle floor into a huge sweatbox. Mitchell knelt in the palms and wiped his stinging eyes as he gazed across the river. Two hours and all he'd found were the tracks of the natural predators of this hell on earth. Two commo checks with B.J.'s group upriver had confirmed that they were having the same kind of luck.

Karpov edged up beside Mitchell, looking up and down the river. He whispered, "What do you think, Sergeant?"

Mitchell wiped his face with the olive drab cravat tied around his neck and was about to answer when he stiffened. He pulled the colonel to the ground.

The men behind them automatically dropped to the prone position, flipping the safeties off their weapons.

Karpov glanced questioningly at Mitchell, then out at the murky brown water of the river that lay in front of them. He didn't see anything.

"Boats!" whispered Mitchell, pointing to the bend in the river. "They're coming this way."

Karpov tilted his head slightly, straining to pick up any sound. He heard nothing. "Are you sure, Sergeant?"

Mitchell nodded. His eyes never left the bend in the river.

"Heavy inboards," he whispered. "River patrol boat more than likely. No—there's two of 'em."

Jake low-crawled up beside the two men. "What we got?"

"The sergeant says we have two patrol boats coming around that bend," whispered Karpov.

Jake raised his head slightly to look over the short grass in front of him. He was about to say he didn't see or hear anything, when suddenly the bow of the first boat appeared, then the second. "Shit!" whispered Jake as he lowered his head. "He's right—they're going to pass right in front of us. We're going to have to move farther back into the jungle. Their bridge is high enough that they'll spot us if we stay here."

The three men had not moved more than a few feet when Sergeant Gorki, his face bathed in sweat, crawled hastily up to the them and anxiously whispered, "Army patrol—behind us. They're coming toward the river."

Karpov and Jake exchanged nervous glances as Jake asked, "How many?"

"Fifteen, maybe twenty," replied the young Russian.

The sense of urgency that hung over the small group of men was apparent. They couldn't stay near the river nor could they fall back far enough to go unnoticed by the soldiers standing on the upper level of the double-decked patrol craft.

Lieutenant Chivenov and Fletcher now joined them. "Kerenski is keeping an eye on the rear, but that patrol is heading straight for us, Colonel," said Fletcher. "Figure we got ten minutes to either shit or get off the pot before they're steppin' on our fingers."

"Two boats," said Mitchell. "Armament, twin fifty caliber machine guns on the bow with an M-60 machine gun on the upper deck. One 40mm cannon on the stern, and the troops are carrying M-16A2s. I count six men per boat, Commander."

Sergeant Gorki added his expertise to the evaluation. "Judging from the three antenna systems on the forward deck, they have both FM and AM capabilities, and a sonar radar system for depth readings. If we have to take these people out, sir, we will have to knock out the antenna systems in the first few seconds of the battle. Otherwise, we are certain to be reported."

Jake and Karpov nodded in agreement.

"Well, gentlemen," said Jake, "I'd say we've run out of options. At the rate the patrol behind us is moving, they'll be on top of us at about the same time the boats are directly in front of us. There is no longer a question of whether we're going to fight, but rather, how. Colonel Karpov, you have more experience at this than I do. How do we play this one?"

Karpov gave Jake a look of appreciation for the compliment before he replied, "Commander, you and Sergeant Mitchell are the Navy experts, you know where you can do the most damage to the boats. I will leave those to you. The rest of us will deal with the patrol behind us. Give me three minutes to move back and set up. Once you engage the boats, the patrol will rush toward the river. We will attempt to catch them in a cross fire, then hunt down and eliminate the survivors."

"Agreed," said Jake. "Three minutes. Good luck, Colonel."

As Karpov and the others pulled back, Mitchell unhooked his pistol belt and LBE, pushing it aside. Jake did the same. Next, they stripped off their shirts, pants, and boots. Removing the knives and 9mm Berettas from the web gear, they eased themselves to the water's edge.

Jake appeared apprehensive as he stared into the murky water.

"What's the matter, Commander?" whispered Mitchell.

"I was just wondering what might be swimming around in there," replied Jake.

Mitchell grinned as he looked at the water then at Jake. "Hell, sir, whatever's in there can't hurt us any more than those 40mm cannons on those boats." Placing his knife between his teeth, Mitch slid silently into the water and began working his way toward the middle of the river. No sooner had Jake entered the water than he saw a seven-foot snake less than twenty-five feet upriver, gliding its way across the water. Suddenly, sitting behind a desk in his father's law office in Philadelphia didn't seem like such a bad idea.

The water was warm. A slight current pushed against Jake's body. Something slithered against his legs, sending a surge of near panic through the Navy commander's very soul and a chill straight up his back. The boats were less than twenty-five yards away and moving steadily toward the two Navy SEALs. Mitchell had moved to the far side of the river, his head barely visible above the water. He would take the first boat, Jake the second. The men on board took no notice of the water, but were scanning the jungle along the banks of the river. Ten yards away now. Five yards.

Mitchell began to flutter kick his way alongside the hull as the ship glided beside him. A ladder attached to the side was the only object he could grab. It was a one-time shot; if he missed, he would be drawn underneath the boat and sliced to pieces by the twin props of the inboards. His hand shot out. He latched onto the bottom rung. The boat's forward progress pulled him along. Using the strength of his powerful arms, the big man pulled himself up by the ladder and hooked his toes onto the last step. Looking back at the other boat, he saw that Jake was no longer in the water. He hoped he was ready. They were running out of time. He saw the top of Jake's head peek over the far side of the second boat. It was now or never.

Taking a deep breath, Mitchell readied the muscles in his legs. Making sure of his footing on the rail, he lifted himself straight up and out of the water. A soldier standing near the rear of the boat stared with disbelief at the bare-chested giant who appeared only inches from him. His mouth opened, but before he could scream, Mitchell lashed out with his knife, cutting a wide gash along the man's throat. Blood spurted and the man's hands went up to his throat in a futile effort to stop the flow.

A second soldier turned just as the SEAL swung over the side and onto the boat. He only managed to bring his rifle up a few inches before Mitchell flipped the knife in the air, caught it by the tip of the blade and sent it sailing the short distance across the deck into the man's chest. The man's rifle slipped from his hands and clattered to the deck as he fell over the side. The three men on the upper deck turned in time to find themselves staring down the barrel of the 9mm Beretta automatic as Mitchell squeezed off a rapid series of nine shots. Every bullet found its mark, sending the surprised men flying backward from the impact. One fell to the lower deck, the other two into the river. That left only one more, but where was he?

Jake swung on board the second ship only seconds behind Mitchell. Two of the men at the rear of the number two boat felt the cold steel of the blade before the shooting started on the first boat. The action on Mitchell's boat had drawn the remaining four men of the second boat toward the front. Jake heard the sound of rifle fire. They were shooting at Mitch. Scrambling up the ladder that led to the bridge, he leaped to the top level, firing. Three of the men fell in a crumpled heap. The fourth swung his rifle at Jake and cut loose on full automatic. The rounds sent a flurry of splintered wood and sparks along the guardrail beside Jake. Mortimer fired from the hip, sending two bullets into the man's chest and knocking him to the lower deck. Jake heard the man's back break as he landed across one of the barrels of the twin fifties.

Grabbing the wheel of his boat, Jake steered it back toward the center of the river. Mitchell's boat was drifting dangerously close to the bank. Jake noticed that there was no one at the wheel.

Mitchell appeared on the lower deck in front of the bridge. Jake could tell by the way the man was moving and holding the Beretta that he still had someone alive on the boat. Tying off the wheel, Jake grabbed up one of the M-16s on the deck. He wasn't sure, but he could swear he saw movement from underneath the wadded-up tarp Mitchell had just passed. Zeroing in on the canvas, he waited until Mitchell was out of the line of fire, then squeezed off four quick rounds.

Mitchell flattened himself on the deck. He stared back at Jake, who was bringing his rifle back up and resting it on the forward rail of the bridge. Getting to his feet, Mitch slowly turned. He spotted the pool of blood that was running out from beneath the tarp. "That's one I owe you, Commander," he yelled.

Jake waved before gunning the engines to pull alongside the first boat. Just as they dropped anchors, the jungle to their right erupted in a roar of automatic weapons fire and grenade explosions. Running to the twin fifties, both SEALs double pumped the arming handles and swung the lethal weapons toward the riverbank. Within minutes, the firefight dwindled to a few shots that echoed through the trees. Three soldiers broke from the jungle and, tossing their weapons aside, leaped into the river, swimming for the patrol boats. Mitchell hesitated as he looked at Jake. These men were totally helpless in the water. It didn't seem right. It was a decision neither man had to make. Snake Adams appeared on the bank and with three well placed shots, shattered all three heads like cantaloupes hit with a sledgehammer.

Jake felt a little sick for a moment, but he quickly recovered as he thought of what those same men would have done had it been Mitchell or him in the water.

Adams waved from the bank. He yelled that the colonel was hiding the bodies. They had gotten them all. Jake told him when they were ready, they would swing along the bank and pick them up.

Adams acknowledged and went back to help the others.

While Mitchell disposed of the bodies on the boats, Jake radioed B.J., giving him details of the action.

Mitchell came topside. The Navy man was smiling like he'd just gotten laid for the first time in his life. Holding out a map in his hand, Mitch tapped an area that had been circled in pencil. It was the exact location of the Medina drug lab. It was eight miles downriver.

Giving Mitch the thumbs-up sign, Jake relayed this new information to Mattson. After Jake picked up the colonel and his team they would move three miles upriver and recover B.J. and his team. Then they would swing back downriver toward the location indicated on the map. They were getting closer, and they knew it. At least now they wouldn't be looking for a needle in a haystack, and what was even better, they moved from the jungle boot express to first class, compliments of the Amazon Battalion Navy.

By noon, both teams had been picked up, and the patrol boats were heading back downriver. Among the items Mitchell found before disposing of the bodies were the primary and alternate frequencies and call signs used by the river patrol and the patrol that had been wiped out by Colonel Karpov. Although a Russian, Gorki spoke flawless Spanish. He volun-

teered to stay below with the radios and handle all the
incoming traffic. So far, they had only received one call from
the base headquarters requesting the location of the boats.
Utilizing the maps in the radio room, the Russian communicator calculated the time and the approximate speed the boats
had been traveling. He quickly figured the distance in nautical
miles and gave them the coordinates where the boats should
have been had they not encountered the two Navy SEALs. The
coordinates given by Gorki were accepted by the battalion base
without question.

B.J. shifted against the wall of the lower deck but still could
not find a comfortable position. When Jake picked them up,
Mattson noticed the tired and beleaguered look on the faces of
the men, who had gone over thirty-six hours without sleep.
Add to that the energy-draining heat and the humidity, and it
was clear that the men needed some rest. B.J. directed Mitchell
to find an inlet somewhere along the river that offered good
concealment form the air and any traffic that might come along
the river. They would hide out for the day, and the men could
get some sleep before the final move on the target tonight.
Although a daytime raid had been mentioned, both Mattson
and Karpov agreed that up to this point, they had used up more
than their share of luck. During the short morning battle, only
Lieutenant Chivenov had been wounded. He had received a
grazing shot along his right rib cage, more painful than serious.
They now had the boats, a definite fix on the location of the
lab, and the entire communications package. No one had any
idea they were there, and B.J. wanted to keep it that way.

Mattson shifted again, but began to realize that for him sleep
was impossible. The small inlet Mitchell had found offered
plenty of concealment, but little air. B.J. wanted to sleep, but
the sultry heat was not about to allow him that luxury. Pulling
himself to his feet, B.J. stretched. The small aches and pains
in his lower back and legs reminded him that they had not yet
forgiven him the atrocious tree landing of this morning.

Looking about the decks of both ships, he began to think that
he was the only one who couldn't sleep. Then he saw Karpov
sitting in the jump seat between the fifties at the rear of the

boat. B.J. figured this would be a good time to ask the colonel about "the star of the czar."

The colonel was apparently in deep thought. He didn't hear B.J. come up behind him.

Mattson pulled a pack of gum from his shirt pocket. He stepped to the side of the machine guns as he held the stick of gum out and asked, "Gum, Colonel?"

Karpov sat up with a start, but quickly recovered. "No thank you, Major."

Mattson wasn't exactly sure of how to go about this. So far, they had been getting along pretty well, better than he ever thought they would. Now he was about to risk all that by insisting that this man tell him what Yelintikov's message really meant, if it meant anything at all. B.J. saw that the colonel's eyes were fixed on a low branch a few yards ahead of the bow of the boat. A palm viper slid slowly, methodically along the thin branch. It's prey, a small tree frog near the end of the limb, was enjoying a feast of ants scurrying across a broad palm leaf. When the snake moved again, the frog, sensing the vibration, stopped and hunched down, readying his powerful legs for a leap to safety. The snake suddenly stopped. Its small beady eyes fixed on its prey. The frog, feeling the danger had passed, went back to his ants. Both Mattson and Karpov were totally involved in watching this game of survival in nature's playhouse.

The snake began to move again. The frog stopped. The snake stopped. This scenario continued twice more, with the snake slowly but surely moving closer. After the third time, the frog was sure there was danger, and he started to make his leap. Then, a furry leaf worm came inching its way along the same branch toward the frog, who spotted it immediately. With the danger momentarily forgotten, the frog's long tongue darted out and snatched up the worm. At the same instant, the snake struck, burying its fangs into the frog's neck, then whipped its long body around its prey in a series of ever tightening coils. Confident that its grip was secure, the snake reared its head back and issued two more bites to the frog's neck in rapid succession. For the frog it was over. His strong legs kicked at the air until finally they stiffened, then went limp.

There was a lesson to be learned there, thought B.J. The frog had chosen to ignore its true senses and the warning signals of approaching danger—just as he, himself was now trying to find reasons to ignore Yelintikov's message to Karpov. There was obviously little advantage to being a frog.

"Colonel, the message I gave you from Yelintikov. What did it really mean?" asked B.J. point-blank without looking at the man whose eyes he could feel on his neck.

"What do you think it meant, Major?" asked the colonel quietly, leaning back in the metal seat.

B.J. felt a slow twisting in his gut. A question for a question response. He was right. There was more to the message than Karpov was telling. It was a code of some type. But what did it mean? B.J. turned, leaned on the barrels directly in front of the Russian, and stared into the man's swollen and blackened eyes. "I have no idea, Colonel, but whatever it means, it has no place in this operation. So far we've been lucky. We've worked well together, and that's only because we've had no secrets from one another. That's the way it should be. Even McGee, right or wrong, was honest about how he felt about you and your people. I'd hate to think that has all changed now, Colonel. Especially with what we have planned for tonight. I'm being straight with you, Colonel. Will you do the same?"

Karpov broke off the eye contact and stared down at the twin triggers of the machine guns. He liked Mattson, as a matter of fact, he liked all the Americans on this team—even McGee. He didn't want to have to lie to this man for whom he had gained considerable respect, but there were some things better left alone. This was one of those things. Looking back up at B.J., he said, "Major, I regret that I can tell you nothing more about this matter. I will, however, assure you that it will in no way affect you or your men."

"Bullshit, Colonel!" exploded B.J. "We work as a team, Alexei. A single, independent action by one renegade member of this team can cost the lives of one or all of us! You know that! So let's cut the fucking crap, okay? We've both been around this business too long to be trying to bullshit each other."

"Very well, Major," said Karpov, fully understanding this man's concern. In less than eight hours, they would be going into a battle where they would be outnumbered five to one. The last thing a leader of that type of operation needs is another problem hanging in limbo. "I give you my word, Major. The message in question has absolutely nothing to do with you or your men. It will have no effect on our mission tonight." Swinging out of the chair, Karpov bowed slightly as he said, "Now, if you will excuse me, I think I will try to get some sleep. I suggest that you do the same."

As he watched the man walk away, B.J. whispered under his breath, "Damn it! I'm going to have to stay close to that man tonight."

CHAPTER 11

Rodrigo Arias had come to see them at 1800 hours. His mood was jovial. The Russians had agreed to their terms. If all went as planned, they would be released within two days. Taking advantage of the man's mood, Captain Longly dared to ask for morphine for Molotov's leg. The wound had worsened during their trip down the river. Gangrene had already set in. The putrid smell was next to unbearable and the creeping poison was leaving a terrible black-and-blue path as it worked its way half the distance up toward the old man's hip. The slightest movement now brought him excruciating pain.

Arias had approached the Russian, but the smell had driven him back. He told her he had no morphine, at least, not the type she would need for the old man. However, he did have something just as good. Tossing her a bag of cocaine, he laughed. "Enjoy, my friends. Celebrate all you want."

Kneeling next to Molotov, Longly placed a small amount of the powder on her finger and held it under the colonel's nose.

Molotov, his tolerance for pain totally destroyed, gladly inhaled deeply the white powder that had meant freedom for his son. In minutes, the pain had subsided, and Molotov's eyes

160

brightened. "He is a fool, you know," he said, laughing quietly as he dipped a finger into the bag and inhaled a larger amount of cocaine.

"Why do you say that, Colonel Molotov?" asked Watson, now kneeling on the other side of the colonel.

Molotov squinted his eyes at Watson as if seeing the black airman for the first time. "How do you know I am a colonel? Oh, of course—you're—you're one of the new men in my unit, that's right. Strange—I don't remember having black men in my unit."

Captain Longly looked down at the elderly man sadly. His age, the terrible wound, and now the cocaine were playing tricks on the colonel's mind. "Medina told us everything, Colonel," said Longly in her quiet, caring voice. "We know about your son, the ether, the shipments—everything."

Fingering another load of the powder, Molotov brought it up before his tired eyes. It seemed so white—whiter than the early snows of the Ukraine winters he'd known as a boy. "Yes! Ether—they needed ether—I needed my son." Moving his finger toward Longly, he continued. "See how pretty it is—so white." A pause, then, "It's a trick you know. They'll be coming for us. They only agreed in order to stall for time. They'll come—you'll see." The finger disappeared up Molotov's nose as he smiled a silly grin.

"Who, Colonel? Who's coming for us?" asked Watson.

"An honorable man that Abdul Khalig—rides a fine camel, you know—yes, he does. Karpov! Yes, they'll send Karpov for us. That would be their choice, because it would be mine as well, you see."

"Hey, Top! Who in the hell is Abdul Khalig?" asked Sergeant Cochran, looking at Watson.

Watson stared back at the boy in disbelief as he answered, "Hell, Cochran, do I look like a damn *Jeopardy* contestant or what? How the fuck do I know who he is? Shit! Who's Karpov?"

Molotov's eyes lit up at the mention of the name. "Alexei— Colonel Alexei Karpov—finest Special Troops commander in Russia. I know. I taught him everything he knows. He is like a second son to me. Yes, it will be Alexei who comes for us."

"When, Colonel? When will he come?" asked Longly.

Raising his calloused, wrinkled hand, Molotov reached out and touched her soft cheek, letting his fingers glide down her face to her chin and back up again, coming to rest at a small lock of hair that hung near her ear. She didn't pull away. She just smiled into the kind and gentle eyes of this man whose rough hands and warm eyes reminded her of her father.

"Soon, my child—he will come soon. I feel it. Such soft skin—Yuri has soft skin, you know—like his mother. Tired— I'm so tired—I—"

Longly held his trembling hand in her own for a moment, then lowered it to the sleeping man's chest.

"You think he knew what he was talking about, Captain?" asked Cochran. "I mean, about this Russian Rambo of his coming after us."

Running her hand gently along the lines of the leathery, weatherworn face of a man whom she was having a hard time envisioning as her enemy, she wiped a tear from her eye and whispered, "I hope so. I pray someone—anyone comes—for his sake."

The clouds passed over the moon, cutting off what little light was available to Mitchell and Mortimer as they cut the engines on the patrol boats and began to drift with the current.

At their present rate of speed, they would be at the unloading docks of the drug lab in approximately fifteen minutes. If things were going as planned, B.J. and Major Suslov, with Adams, Fletcher, Trotsky, and Gorki would be waiting for them. Utilizing two rubber rafts which had been stored on board, they had departed thirty minutes ahead of the patrol boats. B.J. and his people would handle any guards that might be in the dock area. The moon, in its three-quarter stage, reappeared, allowing them the opportunity to navigate toward the center of the river. Colonel Karpov strained his eyes in the darkness, watching the right bank for the twin flashes of light that would signal that the docks had been secured by Mattson and the advance team.

"We should be coming up on the docks any minute now, Colonel," whispered Jake.

Karpov did not reply, maintaining total concentration on the right bank. He stood ready to flip the safety off the AK-47. Suddenly, there it was: two one-second flashes from the small pin light B.J. was carrying. There was a pause, then two more in rapid succession. They had control of the docks.

Clouds blotted out the moon once more, but it didn't matter. Jake was close enough that he guided the big boat alongside the wooden structure as easily as if he were parking a car. Mitchell tossed the tie-off ropes to the men on the docks. They quickly pulled with all their strength, bringing the boat to a stop before it could bump into the rear of Jake's boat.

Colonel Karpov directed Sergeant Kerenski to remain with the patrol boats. If anyone should approach before the shooting began, he was to use his knife. There must not be any shooting before they had a positive location on the prisoners.

Jake disappeared into the commo room.

Taking the remainder of the men with him, Colonel Karpov led them across the docks and into the jungle where B.J. and the others were waiting. The colonel knelt down. Feeling something warm under his knee, he hurriedly rose again. A momentary opening in the clouds provided enough light for him to see the three bodies that lay in a pile next to B.J. Their throats had been cut. Moving to Mattson's side and kneeling, Karpov whispered, "Was this all of them?"

"No," replied B.J. quietly. "There's two more in the river. Adams and Trotsky have gone ahead to scout out the lab. I told them we'd wait for them here."

Karpov nodded his approval as Jake joined them. Mattson could hear the hint of excitement in his partner's voice as the adrenaline rushed in expectation of what was about to happen.

"I talked with Smitty and Ballock. They're scrambling the Hueys for pickup. The Cobras will be flying support, using night vision goggles. Smitty said not worry about that—he checked the pilots out and they're all top guns in the night fire department."

"ETA?" asked B.J.

"They figure forty-five minutes for the Cobras, one hour for the pickup birds," replied Jake.

"Landing zone location?" said Mattson.

"Like we planned, B.J. I told them we'd blow a hole in the area around the lab. Smitty said that wouldn't be a problem."

Adams rejoined the group as Mattson said, "Okay, boys and girls, it's almost game time."

Adams slid in between the leaders and whispered, "Damn big place, B.J. They've got maybe fifty or sixty guys in there, all armed to the teeth. They've got a sixty machine gun mounted on a platform on the west wall. Communications building sits in the center of the place. Another sixty mounted on top of that. Troop barracks are two longhouses to the right of the ComCenter. Couldn't get close enough to tell how many people might be there."

"The prisoners?" asked Karpov.

"We didn't see them, sir, but they have two men guarding a blockhouse that sits next to the main house. I'd be willing to bet that's where we'll find our people."

"Trotsky?" asked B.J.

"Stayed on site to confirm the prisoner location and get an accurate count on the number of people in there. I can lead you in," whispered Adams with the same sound of excitement that had been in Jake's voice.

B.J. looked across at Colonel Karpov in the darkness. He said, "Okay, Jake, you and Snake take them on up and get into position. The colonel and I will be along in a minute."

There was a moment of silence as Karpov looked up, obviously surprised by the order.

"Move out, Jake," said Mattson.

Jake looked at both men, then to Adams, who shrugged his big shoulders.

Turning on his heels, Adams crouched low to begin his return into the jungle brush.

Jake motioned for the others to follow.

B.J. waited until the last man had disappeared before turning to Karpov. "Colonel, I had a talk with Major Suslov while we waited on the dock. I asked him about this 'star of the czar' business. He seemed a little surprised that I would have any knowledge of that subject. Of course, I lied. I told him you and I had talked in great depth about the matter. He freely talked about its meaning after that."

Karpov noted that the earlier anger and frustration in Mattson's voice had disappeared. "So, Major, you know what Comrade Yelintikov's message means, then?"

"Yes, Colonel. We have a little phrase of our own, but then, I'm sure you've heard it before. We're not quite as imaginative as your KGB. We simply say, 'Terminate with extreme prejudice!' You, Colonel, have been asked to kill not only one of your country's heroes, but from what Suslov tells me, a man who is like a father to you. Is that it, Colonel?" asked B.J. sadly. "So much for trust. They were going to kill Molotov from the very beginning. The fact that our people got involved only made things more convenient for the people in Moscow. A joint operation gave you more firepower and increased your odds for success. All very neat and tidy, huh, Colonel?"

Karpov suddenly felt very tired. Mattson had figured it out. Part of it, anyway. Yelintikov, on his arrival in Panama, had made one last appeal on Colonel Molotov's behalf. His message to Karpov was confirmation that the appeal had been rejected. Mattson was right, Molotov was like a father to him, and Yelintikov's order had been honored in Red Square before thousands and had stood with his historic leaders of Mother Russia, had suddenly become an embarrassment. They wanted him "terminated," and Karpov had been the chosen executioner from the very beginning.

"What if I decide not to let you do this thing, Colonel?" asked B.J.

"Is is not your affair, Major. Your primary concern is with your own people. I advise you not to interfere," said Karpov in a bitter and hostile tone. "This matter is going to be hard enough as it is. I would regret having to lose two friends in the same night, B.J."

"Well, we'll just have to see how it plays when the time comes then, won't we, Colonel? I hope you'll change your mind before I have to—"

Jake broke through the brush, cutting off Mattson before he could finish.

"B.J, we got a confirm on the prisoners, but we can't wait any longer. Those assholes are getting drunk. They just brought Pat outside. They're planning on stripping her and then— Shit! I don't have to draw you any pictures, do I? We've got to kick the hell out of them right now, B.J. We can't wait for gunships."

Karpov and Mattson stared across at each other in silence, each wondering in his own mind if he could kill the other if it became necessary.

"B.J., goddamn it, come on!" said Jake as he turned to run back toward the lab and the others.

Mattson glanced at his watch. The Cobras should be twenty minutes out. Jake was right. They couldn't wait any longer.

"What we came for awaits us beyond that jungle, Colonel. Shall we go?" asked Mattson, slapping the bottom of the magazine in his MP-5 to be sure it was well seated in position.

Doing the same to the magazine of his AK-47, Karpov stood and, without answering, began to move through the jungle.

B.J. followed close behind.

They had only gone a few yards when three rapid shots rang out, followed by a long burst of automatic weapons fire.

"Shit!" yelled B.J. as he broke into a run to pass the Russian.

Arias, in a near drunken state, had decided that it was time to finish what he had started back at the Medina ranch. He would have the woman first, then turn her over to his men for their pleasure. He had the Russian deal now, hell with the Americans.

She had been brought out with her shirt and bra torn from her body. Three men held her firmly and fondled her attractive breasts.

Arias had just stepped from the house when Jake squeezed off the three shots that tore through the men holding Longly. She fell to the ground and covered her head as a burst of automatic fire took down three more men standing less than ten yards from her. The ground shook as a wave of grenades sailed out of the jungle, landing in or near the surrounding buildings. Debris rained down all around the terrified woman. Suddenly, she felt hands on her bare back. She screamed.

"Pat! Pat! It's me, Jake. Come on. Get up."

It was like a dream, the familiar voice and the big hands.

She wanted to believe it was Jake, but somehow it seemed impossible that he was here.

The Navy commander pulled her to her feet and smiled into her startled eyes. "Hi, kid. Sorry I'm late. Did you already order the wine?"

She was crying and laughing at the same time. "Oh, Jake." She clung to him in the midst of the gunfire and explosions as if his presence was enough to ward off any threat or danger.

Kissing her cheek, he pulled her along behind him as they made a dash for the cover of the trees.

"My men, Jake. What about my men?"

Pulling the 9mm Beretta from his shoulder holster, he jacked a round in the chamber and pressed it into her hand. "We're going for them now, Pat. You stay here and don't be afraid to use this thing."

He was gone before she could answer. Trembling, she stared out at the blazing buildings and the muzzle flashes of the weapons as men rushed across open ground firing, killing, and being killed.

Three rounds ricocheted off the far wall as Watson and Cochran huddled in the corner near the wall. Someone yelled for them to get away from the door, then fired a short burst through the lock before kicking it open.

The two men looked up. Momentarily confused, they stared at their two rescuers.

Fletcher and Gorki swung their weapons around the room as Fletcher yelled, "Is that Colonel Molotov?"

"Yes," answered Watson as the two airmen moved to the door. "Where's Captain Longly?" asked Cochran.

"She's safe," said Fletcher, stepping out of the door and grabbing two of the rifles from the dead guards beside the door. "Here, take these. You're going to need them. Gorki, we'll have to come back for the colonel. Let's get these guys out of here first."

Sergeant Gorki stared in awe of the legend who lay on the floor across the room.

"Gorki! Come on!" yelled Fletcher as he spun out the doorway. Watson and Cochran were right on his heels.

"I will be back, my colonel," muttered Gorki as he turned.

He was hit across the chest by a burst from the machine gun atop the platform on the west wall. The young Russian staggered back and slumped against the wall. Blood slowly streamed out of the corner of his mouth and the five holes in the front of his shirt. He was dead.

B.J. and Karpov rounded the corner of the main house and came face to face with six gunmen coming right at them. Flipping the switches on their weapons to full auto and firing at the same time from the hip, the two commanders sent all six sprawling into a heap before them. Changing magazines, they leaped over the dead men and pressed themselves against one wall of the house.

Mattson saw Fletcher running across the open ground with the airmen following. Bullets were kicking up the dirt all around them. Fletcher fell to the ground, grabbing at his leg. The black airman knelt down, fired a burst that took out two men running at them, and lifted Fletcher onto his back while the other airman laid down covering fire.

Mitchell and Major Suslov cut down four men at the base of the tower that supported the M-60 machine gun. Slinging his rifle across his chest, Mitchell turned and started up the ladder leading to the platform. He had only made the first three rungs when one of the men on the top looked over the side, swung his rifle out and down, and squeezed off a short burst of automatic. Mitchell pitched back from the ladder. A bullet went through his right shoulder and his right side. Suslov yelled, stepped underneath the wooden tower, and sprayed thirty rounds from his AK through the floor of the platform. The men on top screamed as the bullets tore through their feet and up into their bodies. Two fell, rolled off the platform, and crashed to the ground near Mitchell, who was trying to pull himself to his feet. Suslov ran out to help him. As he knelt down and wrapped Mitchell's arm around his neck, his body stiffened, and a stunned look came over his face. Mitchell could feel the warm blood coming from the hole in the man's back. Looking up, he saw one of the men who had been hit on the tower lower his head and the rifle that he had used to put the bullet into the Russian major's back. The man fell from the tower.

Snake Adams and Lieutenant Chivenov dived behind two

large vats as a line of bullets tore up the ground behind them. Loading a 40mm shell into the 203, Adams raised up and sighted in on the sixty machine gun on top of the main house. Yelling a warning to B.J. and Karpov, he squeezed the trigger on the grenade launcher. The heavy thump of the round being fired rose above the sounds of the small arms fire as the grenade arched its way to the target. The explosion lit up the sky as gun, men, and parts of the roof were sent flying.

"Hot damn! I love this shit!" shouted Adams as he loaded another round and fired point-blank into the front door of one of the longhouses, blowing out windows and sending the men inside scurrying out the lighted doorway where Chivenov picked them off one by one.

"Hey! That ain't bad shootin' for a fuckin' medicine man, Doc," laughed Adams as he reloaded. Chivenov looked up at the American with a show of satisfaction and said, "Colonel Karpov taught me to—" The words abruptly ended as Chivenov was slammed into the side of the metal vat. Adams looked over in time to see the right side of the medical officer's skull explode, splattering him with blood.

"You goddamn fucks!" screamed Adams as he locked the grenade round into place and charged toward the second longhouse, firing. The door exploded and glass shattered as he switched over to the rifle. He ran screaming like a madman through the length of the building, killing eight men by the time he exited the rear door. Breathing heavily, he knelt by a window and slapped another magazine into the weapon. "And B.J. thought I might be too fucking old for this shit." Standing, he started to turn for the corner when he was knocked to the ground by a sledgehammer force that hit him in the back, taking his breath away. The 203 lay only a few feet away, but Adams couldn't feel his hands. He tried to move, but his legs wouldn't work. He was paralyzed. The two bullets had severed his spine.

A pair of white oxford shoes appeared by Adams's head. Looking up, he stared into the eyes of a man with a pencil-thin mustache and a white walking suit. He thought of telling the man he was a little overdressed for this evening's entertainment, but he never got the chance. Arias pointed the gun at the back of Adams's head and fired.

Reloading the pistol, Arias broke for the main house. He had already contacted the Amazon Battalion. They had troops on the way. They would be flown in by chopper and landed at the concealed helicopter pad three yards to the rear of the house. He had only to hide until they arrived.

Leaving Fletcher with the captain, Watson and Cochran, the Air Force medics, ran out to help Mitchell, who was crawling for cover. Heaving the big man onto Cochran's back, they started back when two men appeared to their left. Watson yelled for Cochran to keep going as he whirled to catch one of the men dead in the chest with a burst. The second man fired low and to the right of Watson, who raised his rifle and pulled the trigger. There was an ineffective click. He was out of ammunition, and he had no more magazines.

The man grinned widely as he advanced to the airman, raising his rifle. Watson prepared for the worst.

"Click!" The other man was empty, too.

Watson smiled now, as he screamed, "Your ass is mine, now, boy!" He leaped onto the man. Fists flew as they rolled in the dirt. The man pulled a machete from a bench near a table and swung at Watson, who ducked the blow. Grabbing the man's hand, he pulled it to his mouth and sank his teeth into his palm until he could taste blood. The man screamed and dropped the long lethal blade. Watson grabbed it and turned on his knees. Swinging down with all the power in his big arms, he yelled, "You lose, sucker!" He split the man's head in half.

Karpov and Mattson heard helicopters approaching. Both men tried to listen over the roar of the battle. Then, exchanging worried looks, they knew they had heard the same thing. The helicopters weren't making the right sounds and there were too many of them to be Smitty and the boys.

Grabbing his radio, B.J. pressed the mike switch. "Blue Boy Cobra this is Lonely Blue Boy! Where are you boys? Talk to me, guys. We got a situation here! Over."

Smith's raspy voice came back almost immediately. "Roger, Blue Boy, we see the problem. We got six big ol' Chinook transports just setting down right under us. They're putting troops out about three hundred yards of your two o'clock. We're getting ready to lay the wood to 'em, boss. Then we'll

start on the infantry. Hang loose and stay low. We're coming
in hot. Blue Boy, out!"

Seeing Jake in the trees with the wounded and Captain
Longly, B.J. keyed the radio again. "You monitor that, Jake?"

"Roger! We have everybody but the colonel. They say he's
still in the blockhouse, over."

"Roger! We'll get him. Get in touch with Sergeant Kerenski. Tell him to blow up the boats and join up with you. We'll
go on the same LZ those guys came in on. Out." Turning to
Karpov, B.J. hooked his radio back on his web gear and said,
"Come on, Colonel, there's an old friend waiting to see you."

Both men reached the doorway at the same time. Karpov
flinched when he saw young Issak Gorki's body slumped
against the wall. A moan from inside the room brought the men
inside, their fingers on the triggers of their weapons. There
against the wall lay Colonel Molotov. His gangrenous leg had
swollen to the point of bursting. Now, the raw, red meat of
muscle and tissue mixed with the putrid green of infection lay
open and exposed from the knee to the hip.

"Oh, my God!" uttered Karpov as he lowered his weapon.
He hardly recognized the old man with his sunken eyes, his
haggard face, and wasted body. He had planned to shoot as soon
as he saw the man, but now, seeing him this way, hurt and alone,
he felt tears welling up in his eyes. Laying his weapon aside, he
went over and knelt by the man who had been his teacher.

B.J. realized there was no need for Karpov to have to do the
deed. Molotov was already dead, but was too stubborn to lie
down and let it end.

"You—you came, Alexei," whispered Molotov. "I knew
you would. My—my son— How is he? Is he safe?"

Taking the old man's feverish hand into his own, Karpov
choked back the cry that threatened to break through his
trembling lips. "Yes, Nikolai, he is safe. He—he is anxious to
see you." He felt Molotov's hand tighten around his as the old
man's eyes brightened at the words.

"Oh, to see him once more. But I fear that it is too late for
that now. To know that he is safe is enough—besides—I have
at least lived long enough to see—see one I have always—
thought of—as my other son," gasped Molotov.

Karpov could no longer hold back the tears that now inched their way down his cheeks. He loved this old man with all his heart.

"Do not cry—my son. Even old wolves must die—to make way for the young," whispered Molotov as his body shook and his grip on Karpov's hand tightened. His grip became limp, and his eyes closed. He died.

B.J. heard the muffled sound of crying and stepped out of the doorway to leave the colonel alone with his friend. High in the sky he heard the Cobra gunships begin their run on the big twin engine helicopters that had brought the men of the Amazon Battalion to their deaths. Explosion after explosion rocked the area as the night sky was turned into day by the exploding fuel of the choppers on the ground. Mattson counted six. He knew the mini-guns he heard racking the trees were raining certain death on the soldiers who had come to help their drug dealing friends.

Smith was on the radio, asking for B.J. Unhooking the radio, Mattson was about to press the switch, when out of the corner of his eye he caught a sudden movement at the end of the building. As he turned, he felt a searing pain and the impact of a bullet. He saw the flash as the bullet hit him in the chest and drove him against the door frame. His rifle tumbled from his hands as another pain shot through his leg. The night sky became a dancing kaleidoscope of flashing orange and red lights bursting in his head.

Karpov jumped to his feet and moved for his rifle, but stopped as Rodrigo Arias stepped into the doorway and pointed his pistol at him. Not knowing the colonel was dead, Arias swung the gun toward Molotov and fired twice. The two bullets hit the old man in the chest. Then he pointed the pistol again at Karpov. "Now you see what happens to those who betray the cartel," grinned Arias.

"Go to hell!" snarled Karpov as he straightened up, offering Arias a clear shot at his huge chest.

Three rapid blasts tore the Colombian in half. Karpov threw his hands up to cover his eyes and face from the blood that was splattering the entire room.

"Had an idea that fellow was through talking!" said a

familiar voice as Karpov lowered his hands and saw Hatcher McGee standing in the doorway with his shotgun resting on his hip. "Sorry I took so long in getting here, Colonel. Got a little hot rappelling down that rope out there in the middle of them pissed off dudes. Had to give them a little of that attitude adjustment medicine of yours. Works, too."

Karpov picked up his rifle and stepped up to the big Navy SEAL. "I owe you my life, Commander."

"No, Colonel, I think it's the other way around. I had a lot of time to think after that ass whippin' we laid on each other. You see, I've been alive a long time, but not living. The past can drag a man down sometimes. Well, you made me think about that. I think it's time I started living." Sticking his big hand out to the Russian, he said, "I'd say we're even, Alexei."

Karpov took his hand warmly and gripped it firmly as he asked, "How is Major Mattson?"

"Took one in the leg and one across the chest, but he'll make it okay. He's a pretty tough son of a bitch. You ready to go home?" asked McGee as Smith began circling for a landing.

Glancing back into the room at Molotov, Karpov whispered a farewell as he helped McGee carry Mattson across the compound. It was finally over.

0900 hours—June 26
Gorgious Army Hospital
Panama

B.J. was sitting up in the bed when Jake came in. His chest was still sore as hell, and his leg wound was stiff but healing well. Fletcher and Mitchell were down the hall. They were both already complaining about the food and screaming that they wanted out of the place. Captain Longly and her people were back in Florida. Jake had just come from the embassy. B.J. was anxious to hear what had happened to Karpov on his return to Russia.

"Come on, Jake, quit screwing around and tell me how the Russians are handling this."

Jake smiled as he said, "You're going to love it. Oh, yeah! The general said he would be by to see you a little later. He has checked on you about every hour since they brought you in."

"Fine, Jake. Now tell me! Damn it!"

"Karpov must have done some pretty fancy talking when he got back. The papers are full of the details of the first joint Russian-American operation against terrorists and drug dealers. He convinced the Kremlin that they still needed heroes. They said that Colonel Molotov was killed while leading the Russian team in a noble effort to rescue captured American military personnel. The press loved it, and the Molotov name will forever be preserved in the history of Mother Russia. Karpov sends you his best, and get this: The Russians have invited a senate committee to tour their Special Operations training facility, but only if they'll assure them that Lieutenant Commander Hatcher McGee will accompany the committee. Now, ain't that a trip?"

Mattson laughed as he thought of a senate committee watching the fight he'd seen in the jungle. They'd have a heart attack.

The CNN news was coming on television with their lead story concerning a drug bust in Colombia that resulted in the death of fourteen bodyguards and a prominent member of the Colombian cartel. B.J. stopped laughing and looked at Jake.

"Oh, yeah. I was going to tell you about that. Seems the Brazilian government was so embarrassed by the actions of their Amazon Battalion that they gave Colombia authority to conduct a raid in the disputed territory. Medina and his boys tried to shoot it out and lost. They got 'em all."

Both men turned to the television as the newscaster provided the details of the videotaped shoot-out.

"Carlos Medina and his men refused to surrender and were shot to death by the Special Colombian Drug Unit in a gun battle that lasted nearly three hours. There have been reports that this unit was led by American Drug Enforcement agents. However, the Colombian government has denied these rumors."

B.J. sat upright in his bed as the camera tracked across the area where the dead men lay and focused in on a man in camouflaged fatigues. He was climbing into a jeep with a Colombian colonel. The man waved the camera away and adjusted his sunglasses. He didn't want anyone to see the scars under his eyes.

IN A WORLD ENSLAVED, THEY'RE FIGHTING BACK!

Freedom is dead in the year 2030—megacorporations rule with a silicon fist, and the once-proud people of the United States are now little more than citizen-slaves. Only one group of men and women can restore freedom and give America back to the people:

THE NIGHT WHISTLERS

The second American Revolution
is about to begin.

THE NIGHT WHISTLERS #1: by Dan Trevor
Available October 1991 from Jove Books!

Here is an exclusive preview. . . .

PROLOGUE

Los Angeles, 2030: Seen from afar, the skyline is not all that different from the way it was in earlier decades. True, the Wilshire corridor is stacked with tall buildings, and there are new forms in the downtown complex: the Mitsubishi Towers, a monstrous obelisk in black obsidian; the Bank of Hamburg Center, suggesting a vaguely Gothic monolith; the Nippon Plaza with its "Oriental Only" dining room slowly revolving beneath hanging gardens; and, peaking above them all like a needle in the sky, the Trans Global Towers, housing the LAPD and their masters, Trans Global Security Systems, a publicly held corporation.

The most noticeable difference in this city is a silver serpentine arch snaking from downtown to Dodger Stadium and into the Valley, and in other directions—to Santa Monica, to San Bernardino, and to cities in the south. Yes, at long last, the monorail was constructed. The original underground Metro was abandoned soon after completion, the hierarchy claiming it earthquake prone, the historians claiming the power elite did not want an underground system of tunnels where people could not be seen, particularly since the subways in New York and other Eastern cities became hotbeds of resistance for a short period.

But to fully grasp the quality of life in this era, to really understand what it is like to live under the Corporate shadow, one ultimately has to step down from the towers and other heights. One has to go to the streets and join the rank and file.

Those not lucky enough to inherit executive positions usually live in company housing complexes—which are little more than tenements, depending upon the area. The quality of these establishments varies, generally determined by one's position on the Corporate ladder. All in all, however, they are grim—pitifully small, with thin walls and cheap appliances and furnishings. There are invariably, however, built-in televisions, most of them featuring seventy-two-inch screens and "Sensound." It is mandatory to view them during certain hours.

When not spouting propaganda, television is filled with mindless entertainment programming and endless streams of commercials exhorting the populace to "Buy! Buy! Buy!" For above all, this is a nation of consumers. Almost all products, poorly made and disposable, have built-in obsolescence. New lines are frequently introduced as "better" and "improved," even though the changes are generally useless and cosmetic. Waste disposal has therefore become one of the major problems and industries of this society. A certain amount of one's Corporate wages is expected to be spent on consumer goods. This is monitored by the Internal Revenue Service and used somewhat as a test of loyalty, an indicator of an individual's willingness to contribute to society.

The Corporations take care of their own on other levels as well. Employees are, of course, offered incentive bonuses, although these are eaten quickly by increased taxes. They are also supplied with recreational facilities, health care, and a host of psychiatric programs, including Corporate-sponsored mood drugs. In truth, however, the psychiatric programs are more feared than welcomed, for psychiatry has long given up the twentieth-century pretence that it possessed any kind of workable technology to enlighten individuals. Instead, it baldly admits its purpose to bring about "adjustment"—the control and subjugation of individuals "who don't fit in."

Because this is essentially a postindustrial age, and most of the heavy industry has long been shifted abroad to what was once called the Third World, the majority of jobs are basically clerical. There are entire armies of pale-faced word processors, battalions of managers, and legions of attorneys. Entire city blocks are dedicated to data entry facilities, and on any given night, literally thousands of soft-white monitors can be seen glowing through the glass.

There are also, of course, still a few smaller concerns: tawdry bars, gambling dens, cheap hotels, independent though licensed brothels, and the odd shop filled with all the dusty junk that only the poor will buy. And, naturally, there has always been menial labor. Finally there are the elderly and the unemployed, all of whom live in little more than slums.

Although ostensibly anyone may rise through the ranks to an executive position, it is not that simple. As set up, the system invites corruption. Even those who manage to pass the extremely stringent entrance exams and psychiatric tests find it virtually impossible to move up without a final qualifying factor: a sponsor. Unless one is fortunate enough to have friends or relatives in high places, one might as well not even try. If there ever was a classed society, this is it.

In a sense then, the world of 2030 is almost medieval. The Consortium chief executive officers in all the major once-industrial nations rule their regions with as much authority as any feudal lord, and the hordes of clerks are as tied to their keyboards as any serf was ever tied to the land. What were once mounted knights are now Corporate security officers. What was once the omnipotent church is now the psychiatric establishment.

But lest anyone say there is no hope of salvation from this drudgery and entrapment, there are the national lotteries.

Corporately licensed and managed, the Great American Lottery is virtually a national passion. The multitude of ever-changing games are played with all the intensity and fervor of a life-and-death struggle, drawing more than one hundred million participants twice a week. There are systems of play that are as complex and arcane as any cabalistic theorem, and the selection of numbers has been elevated to a religious experience. Not that anyone ever seems to win. At least, not anyone that anyone knows. But at least there is still the dream of complete financial independence and relative freedom.

But if it is an impossible dream that keeps the populace alive, it is a nightmare that keeps them in line. Ever since the Great Upheaval, the Los Angeles Corporate Authority, and its enforcement arm, the LAPD (a Corporate division) have kept this city in an iron grip. And although the LAPD motto is still "To Protect and Serve," its master has changed and its methods are as brutal as those of any secret police. It is much the same in all cities, with all enforcement agencies around the world under the authority of Trans Global.

What with little or no legal restraint, suspects are routinely executed on the streets, or taken to the interrogation centers and tortured to or past the brink of insanity. Corporate spies are everywhere. Dissent is not tolerated.

And yet, in spite of the apparently feudal structure, it must be remembered that this is a high-tech world, one of laser-enhanced surveillance vehicles, sensitive listening devices, spectral imaging weapon systems, ultrasonic crowd control instruments, and voice-activated firing mechanisms.

Thus, even if one were inclined to create a little havoc with, for instance, a late-twentieth-century assault rifle, the disparity is simply too great. Yes, the Uzi may once have been a formidable weapon, but it is nothing compared to a Panasonic mini-missile rounding the corner to hone in on your pounding heartbeat.

Still, despite the suppression, despite the enormous disparity of firepower, despite the odds, there are still a few—literally a handful—who are compelled to resist. This savage world of financial totalitarianism has not subdued them. Rather, if it has taught them anything at all, it is that freedom can only be bought with will and courage and blood.

This is the lesson they are trying to bring to the American people, this and an ancient dream that has always stirred the hearts of men.

The dream of freedom.

CHAPTER 1

The city was still sleeping when the whistling began. The streets were still deserted, and the night winds still rattled through strewn garbage. Now and again, from deep within the tenement bowels came reverberations of harsh shouts, the slamming of a loosely hinged door. But otherwise there was nothing beyond the echo of that solitary whistler.

For a full thirty seconds Phillip Wimple stood stock-still and listened, the collar of his sad and shapeless raincoat turned up against the foul wind. He looked out at the city with calm brown eyes, his slightly lined face expressionless. He stood as detectives the world over stand, with all the weight on his heels, hands jammed into the pockets of his trousers, his cropped, gray head slightly cocked to the left.

Although not a particularly reflective man, those high nocturnal melodies had always left Wimple vaguely pensive. As to the fragment of some half-remembered tune that continually tugs at one's memory, he had always felt compelled to listen—to turn his tired eyes to the grimy Los Angeles skyline and allow the sounds to enter him.

A patrolman approached, a sleek Doberman of a man in Hitachi body armor and a Remco mini-gun harness. Below, on a stretch of filthy pavement that skirted the weed-grown hill, stood four more uniformed patrolmen. Gillette M-90s rested on their hips. The darkened visors of crash helmets concealed

181

their eyes. Turbo-charged Marauders idled softly beside them in the blackness.

"With all due respect, sir, the Chief Inspector wants to know what's holding us up."

Wimple turned again, shifting his gaze to the distant outline of an angular face behind a smoked Marauder windshield. "Well, tell her that if she would be so kind as to join me on this vantage point, I would be more than happy to explain the delay."

"Sir?"

"Ask Miss Strom to come up here."

Wimple returned his gaze to the skyline. Although the whistling had grown fainter, scattered by the predawn breeze, the melody was still audible: high and cold above the city's haze; dark and threatening in the pit of his stomach.

The woman entered his field of vision, an undeniably grim figure in black spandex and vinyl boots—a full-figured woman, about an inch taller than his five-ten. Her shimmering windbreaker was emblazoned with the Corporate logo: twin lightning bolts enclosed in a fist. When Wimple had first laid eyes on her, he took her as a welcome change from the usual Corporate overlord. Not only was she smart, but she was beautiful . . . in a carnivorous way. He had also liked her fire, her determination, and her willingness to fight for a budget. But that was three days ago. Now, watching her stiffly approach through the smog-choked weeds and yellowed litter, he realized that Miss Erica Strom was no different from any of the boardroom commandants sent down to ensure that the Los Angeles Police Department toed the Corporate line.

"You want to tell me what's going on?" Miss Strom planted herself beside him.

Wimple shrugged, studying her profile: the chiseled features, the red-slashed lips, the hair like a black lacquered helmet. "Ever heard a rattler's hiss?" he asked.

Strom narrowed her sea-green eyes at him. "What are you talking about?"

Wimple extended his finger to the sky to indicate the echo of the unseen whistlers. "That," he said. "That sound."

Withdrawing a smokeless cigarette, one of the Surgeon General–Sanctioned brands that tasted like wet hay, Wimple said, "Think of it like this. We're the cavalry. They're the Indians. Maybe they can't touch us up here, but down there it's a whole different story."

"So what are you trying to tell me? That you want to call this patrol off? You want to turn around and go to bed, because some Devo starts whistling in the dark?" Her deep voice had a masculine edge, a hardness.

Wimple shook his head with a tired smirk. Devo: Corporate catchword for any socially deviate individual, generally from the menial work force. "No, Miss Strom," he said, "I'm not trying to tell you that I want to call the patrol off. I'm just saying that if we go down there now, we could find ourselves in one hell of a shit storm."

Strom returned the detective's smirk. "Is that so?"

"Yes, ma'am."

"Well, in that case, Detective, move your men on down. I can hardly wait."

Long favored by patrolmen throughout the Greater Los Angeles sprawl, the Nissan-Pontiac Marauder was a formidable machine. With a nine-liter, methane-charged power plant, the vehicle was capable of running down virtually anything on the road, and was virtually unstoppable by anything less than an armor-piercing shell. Long and low, it was not, however, built for comfort, and the off-road shocks always wreaked havoc on Wimple's spine.

He rode shotgun beside Miss Strom: shoulders hard against the polymer seats, feet braced on the floorboards, right hand firm on the sissy bar. Earlier, when Strom had given the order to move out, there had been several whispered complaints from the patrolmen. Now, however, as the three-vehicle convoy descended into the black heart of the city, the radios were silent.

"Why don't you tell me about them?" Miss Strom said, easing the Marauder onto the wastes of First Street.

Wimple shrugged, his eyes scanning the tenement windows above. "There's not really much to tell," he replied. "About eighteen months ago, we start getting reports of a little Devo action from the outlying precincts. Vandalism mostly. Petty stuff. Then come July and one of the IRS stations goes up in smoke. After that, we start finding it spray-painted all over the walls: Night Whistlers."

"Any idea who's behind it?"

"Yeah, we've got some ideas."

Strom's thin lips hardened. "So what's been the problem? Why haven't you cleaned them out yet?"

Wimple lifted his gaze to the long blocks of tenements ahead—to the smashed windows and rotting doorways, the grimy, crumbling brickwork and trashed streets. "Well, let's just say that the Whistlers turned out to be a little more organized than we thought." His voice was dull, noncommittal. She gave him a quick look then went back to scanning the street.

They had entered the lower reaches of Ninth Street, and another long canyon of smog-browned tenements. For the most part, the residents here were members of the semiskilled labor force, popularly known as the Menials, officially referred to in ethnological surveys as the Lower Middle Class. Included among their ranks were whole armies of word processors, retail clerks, delivery boys, receptionists, and secretaries. By and large, their lives were measured out in pitiful production bonuses, worthless stock options, and department store clearance sales. They also, of course, spent a lot of time pouring over their lottery tickets, and even more in front of their television screens, watching tedious Corporate-controlled programming. Still, no matter how blatant the propaganda, it was more entertaining than their dull existences.

The radio came alive with a harsh metallic burst from the last Marauder in the line: "Possible six-twenty on Hill."

Six-twenty meant curfew violation—which invariably meant Devo action.

Strom dropped her left hand from the steering wheel and activated the dispatch button on the dashboard. "Let's show them a response now, gentlemen." Then bringing the Marauder into a tight turn, she activated the spectral-imaging screen and switched the infrared cameras to the scan mode.

Wimple, however, preferred to use his eyes. He initially saw only a half-glimpsed vision among the heaps of uncollected refuse: a thin, brown figure in a drab-green duffle coat. For a moment, a single perverse moment, he actually considered

saying nothing. He actually considered returning his gaze to
the bleak stretch of road ahead, casually withdrawing another
smokeless cigarette and keeping his mouth firmly shut. But
even as this thought passed through his mind, the image of the
fleeing figure appeared on the screen.

The radio crackled to life again with a voice from the second
Marauder. "I've got clean visual."

There was a quick glimpse of a sprinting form beneath a sagging
balcony, the sudden clamor of a trash can on the pavement.

Strom powered her vehicle into another hard turn, screech-
ing full-throttle into the adjoining alley. Then, as she deftly
lowered her thumb to activate the spotlight, he was suddenly
there: a wiry Hispanic huddled beneath an ancient fire escape.

Strom activated the megaphone, and her voice boomed out
in harsh, clipped syllables: "Remain where you are! Any
attempt to flee will be met with force!"

The figure stumbled back to the alley wall, glaring around like
a blinded bull. He was younger than Wimple had first imagined,
no more than ten or twelve. His duffle coat was army surplus. His
blue jeans were Levi knockoffs. He also wore a pair of black
market running shoes—the badge of the Devos.

Strom eased the Marauder to a stop alongside the number
two and three vehicles. Then, reaching for the stun gun
beneath the dash, she slipped free of her harness and turned to
Wimple. "Come on, Detective, let me show you what law and
order is all about."

Strom and Wimple approached the suspect slowly. To their
left and right, scanning the rooftops with Nikon-Dow Night
Vision Systems atop their M-90s, were the four helmeted
patrolmen from the backup Marauders. Given the word, they
would have been able to pour out some six hundred fragmen-
tation fléchettes in less than a fifty-second burst—more than
enough to shred the kneeling suspect to a bloody pulp.

Wimple looked at the boy's scared eyes. They kept returning
to the stun gun that dangled from Strom's gloved hand.

Manufactured for Trans Global by Krause-Nova Electronics
in Orange County, the XR50 stun gun had become the last
word on hand-held crowd control. It was capable of dispersing
a scatter charge of nearly fifty-thousand volts, instantly immo-

bilizing a two-hundred-pound man. At closer range, and against bare skin, the pain was beyond description.

The boy could not keep himself from shivering when Strom laid the cold tip of the stun gun against his cheek, could not keep himself from mouthing a silent plea. In response, however, Strom merely smiled, and turned to Wimple again.

"Why don't you see what he's carrying, Detective? Hmm? See what our little lost lamb has in his pockets."

Wimple pressed the boy facedown to the pavement, consciously avoiding the terrified eyes. He then lowered himself to a knee and mechanically began to search. On the first pass, he withdrew only a greasy deck of playing cards, a half-eaten chocolate bar, and a stainless steel identity tag made out to one Julio Cadiz. Then, almost regretfully, he slowly peeled a six-inch steak knife from the boy's left ankle.

"Well, well, well." Strom smiled. "What have we here?"

Wimple rose to his feet, turning the steak knife over in his fingers. "These things don't necessarily mean much."

Strom let her smile sag into another smirk. "Is that so, Detective?"

"It's just kind of a status symbol with these kids. They don't ever really use them. They just like to carry them around to show off to their buddies."

But by this point, Strom had already withdrawn a pair of keyless handcuffs . . . had already released the safety on the stun gun.

She secured the boy's wrists behind his back, then yanked up his coat and T-shirt to expose the base of the spine. Although once or twice the boy emitted a pleading whimper, he still hadn't actually spoken.

"Tell your men to secure the area," Strom said as she hunkered down on the pavement beside the handcuffed boy. Then again when Wimple failed to respond: "Secure the area, Detective. Tell your men."

Wimple glanced over his shoulder to the blank faces of the patrolmen. Before he actually gave the order, however, he turned to the woman again. "Look, I'm not trying to tell you how to do your job, Miss Strom, but this is not going to get us anywhere. You understand what I'm saying? And this is not a safe place for us to be wasting our time."

Strom ran a contemplative hand along the gleaming shaft of the stun gun, then dropped her gaze to the shivering boy. Not looking at Wimple, she finally said, "Detective, I think you should get your men to secure the area before this little brat starts screaming and brings out the whole neighborhood."

She waited until the patrolmen posted on the corner fixed their night vision systems on the balconies and rooftops and chambered clips of fléchettes into their weapons. Then very gently, very slowly, she pressed the cold tip of the stun gun to the boy's naked spine.

"Look—," Wimple began.

"Shut up, Detective," she said, her eyes cold, then lowered her gaze back to the boy.

"Well, now, young man. You and I are going to have a little heart to heart. You understand? A frank exchange of views, with you starting first."

An involuntary shudder crossed the thin, feral face of the boy. "Look, lady, I don't know—"

She clamped her hand to his mouth. "No, no, no. That's not how this game is played, my little friend. In this game, you don't speak until I ask a question. Got it?"

The boy may have tried to nod, but Strom had taken hold of his hair. Then, yanking back his head so that his ear was only inches from her lips, she whispered, "Whistlers, my little man. How about telling me what you know about the Whistlers?"

The boy responded with another frenzied shiver, then possibly attempted to mouth some sort of response. But by this time Strom had released his head, activated the stun gun, and pressed the tip home.

The boy seemed to react in definite stages to the voltage, first arching up like a quivering fish, then growing wide-eyed and rigid as the scream tore out of his body. And even when it stopped, he still seemed to have difficulty breathing, while the left leg continued to tremble.

"Now, let's try it again, shall we?" Strom cooed. "Who . . . are . . . the Whistlers?"

The boy shook his head before answering in spluttering gasps. "Look, lady, I don't know what you're talking about. I swear to God. The Whistlers, that's just something that they write on the walls."

"Who writes it on the walls?"

"I don't know. Just some of the Devos around here. I don't know who they are."

"Just some of the Devos, huh? Well, I'm sorry, young man, but that's just not good enough." And lifting up his T-shirt again to expose the base of his spine, she laid down another fifty-thousand volts.

There was something horrifying about the way the boy's eyes grew impossibly wide as he thrashed on the pavement with another trailing scream. There was also something chilling about the way Strom's lips twisted up in a smile as she watched.

Wimple turned his head away, stared for a moment into some distant blackness. Finally, unable to stand the sobs any longer, he approached again.

"Look, don't you think that's enough, Miss Strom? *Miss Strom!*"

She slowly turned on her haunches to face him, her left hand still toying with the boy's sweat-drenched hair. "You got a problem, Detective?"

Wimple met her gaze for a full three seconds before answering, a full three seconds to taste the woman's hatred. "Yeah," he finally nodded. "I got a problem. Quite apart from my personal objection to this activity, I'd like to point out that you are seriously endangering my men. If you think that this neighborhood is asleep right now, you are sadly mistaken. The people up in those buildings know exactly what's going on down here. They know exactly what you're doing, and I can assure you that they don't like it."

She withdrew her fingers from the boy's hair, and his head lolled back to the vomit-smeared pavement. "Well, now, that's very interesting, Detective. Because, you see, I *want* them to know what's going on here. I *want* them to hear every decibel of this little bastard's scream and remember it—"

"Shut up!"

"How dare you tell me to—"

"Shut up and listen!" Wimple said, as the first cold notes of the solitary whistler wafted down from the blackened rooftops.